VOLUNTEER...SPY?

by Dara Carr

VOLUNTEER...SPY?

by Dara Carr

Harrison House Publishing

San Antonio, Texas

Volunteer . . . Spy?
v2.0
Editing by Betty Powell, Linda S. Carr, and Jeff L. Carr
Cover Art designed by Eric A. Carr

Harrison House Publishing
www.theharrisonhousepublishing.com
info@theharrisonhousepublising.com
ISBN: 978-09861285-3-0
Library of Congress Control Number: 2015942425
Harrison House Publishing and the "HH" logo are trademarks belonging to Harrison House Publishing.

PRINTED IN THE UNITED STATES OF AMERICA

FORWARD

When you read through the story you may find several places where the laws of the land do not jive with what is being said. When I look at other stories, be it in movie, a book or television, I have found that some authors will use "Poetic License" to change things to fit their plot. If you watch the movie, "Liar, Liar," there is a glaring discrepancy where the law does not fit the outcome of the court case. If the proper legal decision were used in the movie it would ruin the plot (plus it might give a lot of minors an idea of how to try to get away with something). In "Star Trek" and "Quantum Leap" they constantly misused the laws of physics. A Certain US Senator said that he was being fired upon by the Khmer Rouge, while he was in Viet-Nam, even though that political group did not appear on any political scene until after the USA was out of Viet-Nam. If other authors of fiction and science fiction can use it - so can I. If a United States Senator can boldly get up and be some kind of historical revisionist then who are you or anyone else to say that I cannot. If you try to say that I cannot improvise, revise or use poetic license, then all I have for you is a very loud, sloppy raspberry.

ACKNOWLEDGMENTS

A grateful thanks to a friend Richard L. Roynon Jr. for his constructive criticism. A special thank you to Jeff L. Carr for his assistance, without your support this could not have been possible.

VOLUNTEER...SPY?

1

Several people walked into a conference room. Other than a pull down map of Eastern Europe and western Asia on one end of the room it all looked rather sterile. There was an empty chair at the head of the table. All of the people found a place to sit in one of the many rather uncomfortable looking chairs that lined each side of the long conference table. A man in a rather drab looking brown suit walked in and placed a folder in front of each person at the table. The folders were all marked "Top Secret" in large red block letters. The brown suited man then departed.

Another tall man wearing a dark suit, with dark eyes, very close trimmed brown hair and somewhat of a permanent scowl on his face walked in and sat at the end of the table. He looked around at each of the faces of the other people at the table. He pulled some papers out of his inner jacket pocket, unfolded them, looked them over with a few glances and then finally spoke with a deep voice: "Good morning folks. My name is Colonel Samuel Bates. I am in charge of this operation. You may open your folders and read them at this time."

The sound of tearing paper filled the room as each one broke the seal on their folder and they opened them. Each one sat silently reading. As each one finished, they set the folders back down and looked to the head of the table.

When all of them were finished Colonel Bates spoke again: "This is what we have found out so far. As you can see, it is somewhat incomplete. We are going to have to send some people in. They're going to have to get the rest of the information from any and all of our contacts on the other side."

A rather lean man with a scraggly mustache spoke up: "All of us? Are you going to send all of us in…at the same time?"

"No," said Bates. "Initially we are going to send in just three. Hopefully one of them will get what we need and we won't have to send anyone else. This information is important enough that…we need it…no matter what. If the first ones don't make it back…then we'll have to send in more and more, until we get what we need. Of course, each person that follows later, will be in even greater danger than the previous ones, because our opponents will be aware of and looking for any more new faces."

A heavily muscled man with a shaved head scoffed. "So how do we go about contacting those inside – if they're already looking for us – without arousing any further suspicions?"

"Each one of you will have to set up your own method of getting in and getting out. I don't want to know how. Whoever you contact…if you are caught…I will know of your capture and will inform the others who follow…which contacts are no longer available."

Another man with a large scar across his forehead grunted in disgust. He looked to the head of the table. "My luck has just about been used up. Since the least amount of danger goes with the first group – I am either in the first group or not at all."

Bates looked down at the folder in front of the man. "You haven't been chosen for the first group."

"Then...as I said: I am not in it."

Bates sighed and nodded. "Leave the folder, leave the room and you will discuss this with no one."

The man with the scar stood up. "Yes, Sir, I know the drill," he said without emotion. He closed the folder and departed the room by the most direct route.

"Are there any other objections or observations?" asked Bates. Everyone looked around at the other people in the room. After several moments of silence Bates spoke up again. "There are three of you, who have an orange tab on your folder. You are the ones who will go in first. If you do not have an orange tab you may leave the room...now."

Most of the people stood up and departed. The three that remained, glanced at each of the others who were still there. One was a thick necked man with short brown curly hair and gray eyes that looked somewhat dull. The second was a very small man who looked like he had come from the Greek Islands. The third was an attractive woman with blonde hair, dark eyebrows, very dark eyes and was not ashamed to show a lot of cleavage.

"Any reason the three of us were chosen to go first?" asked the Greek.

"No," said Bates flatly. "The orange tabbed folders were randomly placed in the stack. I didn't want to choose anyone in particular and give any appearance of favoritism. It was total luck of the draw."

"So what are our orders now?" asked the thick neck.

"As I said, you pick your own way in behind the iron curtain. I don't want to know…how or when. Get in, find your contacts, get what information you can, get out and report it. If the information that you have obtained is incomplete, we'll have to continue with others, until we have the complete picture. Until we get all of it, we can't stop. The only deadline is that you three have one month to make your individual plans and execute your departure."

The woman snickered. "Are you saying that I have a free ticket on how *I* plan my mission?" She cocked her head to the side with a provocative grin.

"Exactly," said Bates emphatically. "You make your own plan. I don't want to know about it…unless there is something that you need me to obtain for the complete and proper execution of your plan. Only you know all of it. This way…if there is a leak somewhere…on our side…that leak will not know who is going or when or where. I've done everything I can to make sure that no one else knows about this mission in any way, shape or form. There are those that know of the incomplete information, but they will not know who or how many have gone in to get the rest of the information. If I do find out the worst…then I will know that I need to send someone else. I have been informed that we must get the information…no matter what the cost."

The three Field Agents again read the information that they had thoroughly. They had to memorize it and then leave the file folder behind. Thick neck was the first to leave. He closed the folder and left without any ceremony. The Greek finished reading, sniffed, closed the folder and departed quietly.

The blonde looked at Colonel Bates. "Colonel, once again, are you telling me that I have a free ticket to do anything that I want in order to accomplish this mission?"

"Well I do have to say that it must be within reason, but, with the importance that they're putting on it...try not to break too many laws."

She snickered. "German or American?"

He gave her a bit of a stern look. "We *are* in Germany right now and we don't need any international incident, so if you have to do any...law-breaking...try not to implicate this office." He cleared his throat. "That question makes me feel rather uncomfortable."

"Okay then, I won't tell you anything...yet." She smiled. She got up and sashayed out of the room with a somewhat evil grin on her face.

Bates stood up. He walked around the table collecting all of the folders. He walked back to his office and ran all of the folders through the shredder. He took the shreds, placed them in a burn bag and called his Aide.

The Aide walked in. "Yes, Sir?"

"Burke, this burn bag has top priority to the furnace."

"Yes, Sir."

After Burke departed, Bates sat there wondering if he was sending any of his field agents to their death. He had lost people before, however, this one could be disastrous. The Russians obviously knew how important this was and could be upset and dangerous if they lost control of this situation.

2

The blonde drove home. She walked into her apartment on Homberger Landstrasse. She sat there pondering which identity she would use to start this case. Use one to start it and another to execute it. That plan had worked several times before, so why not do it again? But which one? She hit two hidden locks and her "special" closet opened up. There were several US military uniforms along with numerous European military uniforms. There, on the hanger, was the US Air Force officer's uniform that seemed to be beckoning her. Rhein Main Air Base was close by and she usually found a good fall guy from among military personnel, whenever she had needed one. She had always used them for missions around Europe…on this side of the iron curtain – never on the Soviet side. There were five times as many US Army personnel in the area of Frankfurt, Germany, however, Army personnel were usually in better shape… and might be prone to attempting some kind of retribution. They would fall easier, however, they usually came back swinging. Air Force it is.

She pulled the Air Force uniform out and chose the rank of Major. Major is a good rank. It is enough to scare most people, but not high enough to arouse too much suspicion. Captain or lower might not be enough and anything higher could attract too much unwanted attention. She checked the appropriate Air Force regulation on how to put the Major's oak leaves on. After putting the gold oak leaves on the collar, she turned to her other little trick machines. She needed a military identification card and an identity.

She needed military orders that looked official. That took a little while longer typing them up because she could not afford to have any typographical errors on it.

What name is to be used? Johnson, Jones and Smith were too common. She chose Walker instead. Now a first name. Mary or Anna? No, Marie. So she was going to be Major Marie Walker. She pondered on a middle initial…for about twenty seconds. She decided against it because the less information there was, the fewer the questions…plus forgetting a middle initial in any signature could cause unwanted problems.

Now she needed to get into the main personnel office in order to find what she needed. She cut a set of orders that would get her into the Consolidated Base Personnel Office (CBPO), as a member of an Inspector General (IG) Team. She set it up so that she could get in the office and get into any record that she wanted. Hopefully no one would question her until she had what she wanted. If she could intimidate them enough then no one would have the guts to ask any questions. Fear of failing an inspection was usually enough to accomplish the desired trepidation on their part.

Once she had the orders set up, she started checking to see when the last IG Team went through the Rhein Main CBPO. The last thing she needed was to butt in on an active IG Team inspection. That could bring her party to an unfortunate end that she would not be able to explain without some severe consequences.

After getting all of the paperwork ready, she put the uniform on and stood in front of a mirror checking her appearance and comparing it to the proper regulation. She did several practice salutes as well.

When she was satisfied with costuming and paperwork, she checked on her motor pool. She had to have something that came straight out of an Air Force Base Motor Pool. If she were to show up in a personal vehicle, that could raise some suspicions. She had to check and see if there were any special things about the vehicles that flagged them. The only flag that she found, with a sedan, was that a General of Colonel's staff car had a white roof. All other sedans had a blue roof with no special markings other than those of the Air Police fleet.

She then called Bates on the phone and told him that she might need a little backing for her plan. He listened to the part of her plan that he needed to know and promised that he would back her as far as he could.

After hanging up the phone, Bates sat there wondering what she had in mind. She would be going behind the iron curtain, why did she need carte blanche at a local Air Base? He hoped that she was not abusing the system.

Once she had all that she needed, she headed for the base. Getting through the main gate at Rhein Main Air Base was no problem. An officer driving a military sedan was not questioned. She checked her map of the base and headed for CBPO.

She pulled in and found that there were several spots reserved for military vehicles only. She headed inside with all of her paperwork and was confronted by the Officer in Charge (OIC) – a Major Baldwin - who did not like what he was seeing or hearing. He called and got Colonel Bates on the phone. After getting a chewing out from Bates, he grudgingly allowed Major Walker the freedom she wanted in the file section of the CBPO. Considering Baldwin's anxiety over the situation, she knew that she had to get what she needed quickly and possibly concoct a new line of nonsense…just in case.

It took nearly two days of searching before she finally found three possible candidates. She got as much information from the files that she could afford to take out and got ready for her departure.

She walked into Major Baldwin's office. "Good morning, Major, I'm satisfied with what I've seen," she said cheerfully.

He stood up. "Just exactly what were you looking for? Do you mind telling me?"

She shrugged. "Well, you know how it is - the *need to know* basis."

He glared at her. "I am the head hauncho here. Do NOT try to tell me that I do NOT have a *need to know*, in MY office, where I am the Commander!"

'Oops,' she thought. She smiled. "You're absolutely correct. This is your office. Okay, we heard rumors about this office that raised a few red flags. I came here to check them out. You know, check for any validity of the alleged complaints. Well, it turned out to be a red herring instead of a warning."

He slammed his fist onto his desk. "NOT enough information!"

Now she got a little stern. "I'm very sorry, Major, but I have to report back to my superiors before I can give you any more information." She sighed. "Unfortunately, I was not given enough to give you a full briefing. You know how some of these high ranking types like to keep their secrets in order to make sure that they are the most important one in the situation. I will have to give a report to Colonel Bates, as well as a few others, and then they will give you the information that you need...once everything has been finalized. I'm sorry, but that's all that I can tell you at this time."

She left quickly, knowing that this guy might start harassing Bates. She knew that she was going to have to act fast. She made another phone call to Bates to let him know that there might be a few more phone calls from Baldwin.

Candidate number one turned out to be a bust. This guy was a bit of a trouble maker and was being thrown out of the Air Force. His final information had not been received at CBPO yet, however, he was being sent to Dover Air Force Base in Delaware to be processed out of the Air Force with a less than honorable discharge. He would be leaving, with an escort, in two days.

The second candidate had several had several mediocre performance reports. He had also been given a mediocre report on his physical condition. He was supposed to run 1.5 miles in 12 ½ minutes or less. He had completed the run at 12:37. He was also just a few pounds under his maximum allowable body weight. He was being sent to the gymnasium, under orders, to *get in shape*...or else.

The third candidate was another complete loss. He was in confinement, awaiting a court martial for...what difference did it make? He was in confinement – back to candidate number two.

Back to candidate number two: Sergeant Bradley Franklin Dooley. She snickered. This poor fool had been targeted from the beginning. What were his parents thinking of when they gave him (what she considered) three last names. He was from some small town in Georgia that she had never heard of. Virtually everything that she had read on him summed him up in one word: Substandard. Nobody would miss this yokel, if he turned up…missing.

She checked where he lived. He was in the barracks on the second floor. She would have a tough time getting into the male living quarters, without some kind of justification. That could or would have surely raised some suspicions and unwanted publicity. Many colleges, back in the United States, were going co-ed with their dormitories. The military still remained rather strict about the living quarters for the different sexes among single personnel.

She drove back to her apartment and her "special tricks closet" in order to rearrange a few things. She kept the name, however, she changed the rank. She went from Major to Airman First Class. She left the military sedan and switched to a rusty looking VW Beetle. She put the appropriate stickers on the VW and changed her military ID card as well.

She headed back to Rhein Main Air Base and once again got through the main gate without any problems. She went to the Recreation Center where most of the lower ranking people went to unwind, play billiards and sometimes act generally stupid. This was the hangout for all of the people who could not afford a car but still wanted to have a little entertainment, outside of the barracks.

She looked carefully at a picture that she had obtained of her mark and started wandering around the Rec Center. He was not the best looking man she had ever seen. She was looking for a man who was 22 years old (5 years younger than her), 5'9" (3 inches taller than her), 179 pounds (nearly 60 pounds heavier than her), brown hair, blue eyes...and a lot of pimples.

She went through rooms full of Ping-Pong tables, billiard tables, rooms where some were playing Pinochle, Hearts, Spades and a few other card games and a room where some were playing board games. Everywhere she went, there was the smell of cigarettes, cheap cigars and beer.

She had decided not to wear a uniform in the Rec Center, because most of the people who came in here were in civilian clothing. During her trek through the Rec Center, she crossed paths with several young, arrogant, *self-appointed* studs, who were a little too proud of themselves. Apparently the shorts and tube top were a little too alluring for some of the egomaniacs. She had to turn down several propositions. She noticed that of all of the females in the Rec Center...she was wearing the least amount of clothing. Maybe that was why she was getting so much unwanted attention.

If she had not been totally focused on finding this guy Dooley, she would have stopped and given a few black eyes or maybe even a few ruptures, just to knock them down a few rungs on their ladders. She could not, however, afford that kind of attention being drawn to her. Her provocative clothing was already doing too much of that.

She was just about to give up for the day, when she saw a very sweaty man coming in the main entrance, dressed in a sweatshirt, jeans and tennis shoes, who looked like her target. According to what she saw in the picture, he was not handsome. The problem was that the picture was somewhat complimentary. She had to disguise her disgust as she headed towards Dooley. As she got closer, she was somewhat pleased with the fact that he had done something to clear up most of his acne problem.

She headed towards Dooley and was intercepted by another jerk. This self-indulgent fool was obviously very young. He was over 6' tall and had short brown hair, with dark brown eyes. The way he had his left hand on his crotch, as well as the cocky grin, told her that this was another megalomaniacal idiot with an enormous penile fixation. She grunted with disgust as he started that moronic advance that she would have absolutely no problem turning down.

He walked directly into her path. "Hey baby, How ya doin'?"

She gave him a disgusted look. "My name ain't baby!" She tried to walk around him.

He again moved into her path. "Oh come on, good lookin', don't be mad. I got somethin' here that you should get acquainted with."

"What, your childishly egotistical imagination?"

He gave her a somewhat phony laugh. "Come on back to my room and I'll show you somethin', the likes of which, you ain't never seen."

He moved his hand away from his crotch. She quickly grabbed his manhood and squeezed as hard as she could. He let out a loud wheeze in shock. She was amazed that anyone could open their mouth as wide as he was currently doing. She had never seen a gaping maw that big on any human being before.

"Let's see…I can get all of your stuff in one hand. So that tells me that my baby brother has more stuff than you do." She let go and he fell to his knees groaning and wheezing in pain.

She left the fool and headed for Dooley. He was sitting at a table finishing a can of beer. She sat down next to him. He was oblivious to all that had happened around him. He started working hard on a second can of beer.

"Hi," she said. "Had a hard day?"

He jumped slightly and looked at her. He glanced around and then stared at her in confusion. His body convulsed a little and he cut loose with a long loud belch.

She hid her revulsion with a strained smile. "What's the matter, got nothing to say?"

He leaned back still looking confused. "Who are you?" He had a deep gruff voice.

"I'm someone who has a similar problem to yours."

He looked her up and down quickly. "What're you tryin' to give me? You're not close to being overweight," he said in a disgusted manner.

"No, I can't run worth a hoot."

"Okay, so what?"

"Well, maybe we can work together and try to get up to speed."

His eyes narrowed. "What do you really want?"

"Doing any of this stuff, by yourself, is boring. If you have someone working with you, then it helps things go smoother. So, what do you say?"

He looked at her with suspicion. "You're a girl. I don't trust girls. I've had too many girls lie to me, at me and about me. Sorry, go find someone else to bother."

She gritted her teeth. "What would you say, if I was told by someone, with a higher rank, that I *have* to work with you?"

Now he looked at her incredulously. He closed his eyes and shook his head. He belched again. He looked off at nothing in particular and took another sip of beer. He looked back at her with a somewhat angry glare. "Who?"

"Who...what?"

"Who told you that you have to work with me?"

She felt a pang of frustration. "I can't tell you...right now."

He scoffed. "Proper translation: You're a liar!" He took another long drink from his beer that finished off the can. He looked at her and belched again.

"Look, I need to talk to you, somewhere else. I need to talk to YOU!"

He sighed. "What about?"

"I'll tell you when we're somewhere else."

"Give me a reason to trust you."

"What makes you think that you can't?"

"You're female! That's enough for me to NOT trust you."

The tall punk, that she had disabled, had recovered – slightly. He made an awkward, bow-legged walk to the table where she was sitting with Dooley and sat down. He glared at her. "That was NOT cool!" He was rubbing his crotch and his breathing as a little strained.

She gritted her teeth. "Hey, dummy...do you want a second helping?"

He glared at her and then looked at Dooley. "Hey you, get lost. I gotta talk to this broad."

She leaned forward and scowled at him. "What's your rank? What's your name?" She leaned back and raised her leg under the table, cocked and ready to kick him...where it would count the most.

"The name's Chet Lund! I'm an Airman! Any more questions...baby?"

"You are an Airman. "I'm an Airman First Class. Dooley here is a Sergeant. You are an E-2 mosquito wing and got no authority to give anyone orders except a slick-sleeve...dummy! You get lost!" She was starting to get a little exasperated over how she was losing control of the situation. Then she started wondering if she ever did have any control. One man was a misogynist, while the other was an immature moron with delusions of sexual grandeur. What do you do now?

Lund glared back. "Rank don't mean nuthin' right now. We're off duty here. You got no authority over me like I got no authority over you. Right now, I'm tellin' *him* to get lost cause he's nuthin'."

She scoffed. "Tell that to the Base Commander and/or your Squadron Commander, dummy. I came here to talk to him, not some megalomaniacal idiot with a penile fixation. Now, unless you want a second helping…SCRAM!"

Dooley had been sitting there shaking his head. He stood up. "I don't need this crap. I'm outta here." He started walking away.

She started to get up with Dooley. Lund grabbed her arm and tried to hold her back. She still had her leg slightly cocked and now pulled the trigger. She got Lund right between the legs. He let out a pained grunt and tried to get up. All he could do was fall back into the chair, lay his head on the table and moan with both hands on his groin.

She got up and caught up with Dooley. "Look, man, I need to talk to you. Leaving is a good idea, because we don't need any side show freaks like that jerk."

He gawked at her with his mouth wide open. "Sister, you are trouble! Trouble is something that I don't need! Don't need it now or ever. I'm going back to the barracks and I don't need an escort or follower. Go away and leave me alone!" He quickly headed into a hallway that led to the rear entrance.

She almost had to run to keep up with him. If she didn't get this fool, she would have to go back to CBPO and find someone else. Two days had been used up thus far and she could not afford to waste any more time. She caught up, grabbed his arm and spun him around. "Look, buster, I was told to get with YOU! That jerk back there is…nothing. If he's trouble…fine, we get away from him… avoid him, but I need to talk to you."

He rolled his eyes, stared at the ceiling and huffed. "Tell me who sent you and why and I might consider it. Until then…I'm gonna make like an alligator and drag my tail out of here...alone! That means...without *you*."

Somehow, at that time, Lund caught up with them, even with that very awkward staggering way of walking. She had had enough of his childish attitude and interference. He had grabbed at her to say something and she immediately gave him an elbow to the stomach. He bent over as a result and she gave him a knee to the chin that almost knocked him completely down, falling backwards. She stomped hard on his left foot. He bent over again to grab at the injured foot and made a perfect target out of his face. A hard round house kick to the side of his head made him crumple to the floor like a rag doll. After he fell, the only thing moving was his chest as he lay there unconscious but breathing.

Dooley was staring at her in horror and shock.

She huffed angrily. "Now! I wanted to do this the easy way. With all this, I can't! I need you to come with me – NOW!"

"ARE YOU CRAZY? I have no idea who you are and... the way you just clobbered that guy, what makes you think that I'm stupid enough to hang out with a psycho, kung-fu broad like you?"

She let a small growl loose out of her throat. "An Airman has just been assaulted here in the Rec Center. You stay here and I'll make sure that you get implicated in that assault. I'm sure that he'll agree with *that* because he won't want to admit that he got his butt kicked by a...broad! You come with me and neither of us was anywhere near it – you got that?"

He looked back and forth in the rear hallway. Amazingly, no one else was in this hallway at the time. No one had witnessed the "assault" – except for the two conscious people who were currently standing here. He looked at her sternly. "Where are we going?" he spat through his teeth.

She grabbed his hand and led him out of the Rec Center to her car. After nearly having to force him into the car, she silently drove off the base to a different place that she had in mind. Traffic built as they neared Frankfurt. The city streets were the usual traffic jam of any large city, however, she was used to it.

"We need to do a little bit more of getting into shape and I know a place where we can start. I have something else in mind as well and I'll tell you about it later."

He sat there brooding. "Somehow, I find it impossible to believe you."

She gave him an angry side glance. "Why is it so hard for you to believe me?"

"You're female, you're breathing and you're awake. That means you can't be trusted. All my life, broads like you use me for some…rotten purpose of your own. Why don't you just get it out now…what you want and why?"

She sighed. "Just hang with me right now. We'll get to where we need to be with less problems that way." She pulled up into the gate of one of the many US Army Posts that were scattered all over Frankfurt. She drove directly to the gymnasium and parked. "We're going to do a little workout here," she said cheerfully.

He held his hands out looking totally confused. "What's wrong with the gym at Rhein Main? Why did you bring us here…

to a *grunt* gym on a *grunt* base?"

"No one knows us here. We don't have to worry about anybody from your Squadron or mine giving us a hassle here."

He went limp in the car seat. "You think that that is gonna make a difference? Grunts are even more over-sexed than Air Force! You're gonna get hassled even more...here."

She smiled. "No, it's different here."

He shook his head. "You'll see. All we need is another creep...like the one you knocked silly...and the whole thing starts over again."

They got out of the car and walked into the gym. Inside it smelled badly of sweat and mildew. There was a basketball court to the left. On the right there was a boxing ring and numerous stations for different types of weight lifting. There was also a very large mat where two men were practicing some judo moves.

She looked around with a smile on her face. "Where shall we begin?"

He looked skyward and shook his head. "Why don't we start where we have our problem – on the track?"

She gave a sheepish little laugh. "Oh. Of course. That's out back." She started towards the other side of the gym. She looked back and saw that he was still standing there with his arms folded across his chest. She went back and grabbed his hand. "Come on," she said impatiently.

He hung his head and went with her grudgingly.

They walked out the rear door to the track. It was a standard quarter mile track with eight clearly marked lanes. She was grateful that there were very few people on the track at this time. She started a slow jog and again looked back at him. He was staring off to the side shaking his head.

"Come on!" she said more forcefully.

He gave her a nasty look and started walking. She fell in beside him.

She tried to be friendly by smiling. "We're supposed to be running."

"You can run. I'm walking," he said with a deadpan look.

"Why aren't you running?"

"Not until you tell me what's going on."

She now had a strained smile on her face. "We are trying to get in shape." She found it difficult to talk to him, considering he was being a hard person to talk to, let alone interact intelligently.

"Sure, sure, sure," he muttered as he continued walking.

She huffed at him. "If you're going to continue to walk, you have to do it in the outside lanes of the track."

He immediately did a hard right turn to lane 8, then hard left and continued trudging along.

She walked with him for three silent laps and then said: "I just remembered, I have to make a phone call."

He acknowledged her statement with a disinterested grunt.

"There's a phone box at the end of the track - I'll use that one."

"Why is there a phone out here?" he asked confused.

"If someone goes down on the track, you don't have to waste time running inside in order to call an ambulance," she stated in a matter-of-fact manner. This seemed to be the only way to deal with him - so far.

"Whatever," he sniffed.

She left the track when they got to the phone box. He continued on. She opened the box, picked up the phone and dialed Bates. A different man answered the phone. She gave instructions that she needed special orders cut for Dooley. He was to be assigned Temporary Duty with her – for an unspecified length of time. She also gave a few more instructions on what she needed. The man on the other end seemed a little confused at the other orders. She assured him that he should check with Bates if he had any questions about the what, why or how. She finished the long phone conversation and hung up.

While she was talking on the phone she watched Dooley finish two more walking laps. On the third trip around she joined him again. "Still walking I see," she said trying to be a little encouraging.

"You still haven't told me what's going on – I see," he said flatly.

They walked on in silence. Every now and then, she had to do a quick little run to catch up with him. His strides were longer and more forceful than hers. As they finished the fourth mile, she grabbed him and stopped him. "I thought you were supposed to be out of shape."

He looked down his nose at her. "I can't run. Nobody said that I can't walk." He turned and continued walking. He continued glowering and went back into the concentration of the walk.

She shrugged and sighed. She caught up to him. She decided to see just how far he was capable of going. She counted the laps. 17, 18, 19, 20. A full five miles and he was showing no signs of slowing. 21, 22, 23, 24, 25, 26, 27, 28…she stopped him again. He was still showing no signs of wear and tear while she was sweating profusely and her feet hurt. "How come you don't walk the aerobics? You can walk forever. Have you tried the walk?"

He looked up and sighed. "Have *you* ever tried the walk?" He looked down his nose at her again. "In order to do the walk – in the time allotted – you have to walk at a *brisk pace*. You have to go three miles at a *brisk pace*. Have you ever tried that *brisk pace*? It's impossible to do it without running every now and then. The walk is harder than the run."

"So where did you get the capability of walking…forever?" She was a little winded and was panting a little with a rather dry throat.

He had a totally disenchanted look on his face. "Back home, we lived just outside of town. I had to walk to school for all twelve grades. The elementary school was six miles away, the junior high was five miles away and the high school was eight miles away from home. Rarely, did I get to ride or drive at all. My four sisters had

that privilege. When I got into Basic Training, hey guess what –
we marched. I got to Technical School and guess what – more
marching. Now, I'm at Rhein Main. I have no car because I can't
afford one. I walk. Any more stupid questions Miss Buttinski?"

She sighed in frustration. "Are you ready to leave?"

He grunted. "I never had any reason to come here in the first
place," he said flatly.

"Come on, let's go." She huffed in disgust. Usually all she
had to do was give a coy smile to a man and she had him wrapped
around her little finger. This guy was going to be a real challenge.
She knew that she had to go with him because of all the personnel
files that she had looked through, there was no one else that she
thought she could...abuse. She had spent too much time on this one
to stop now.

On the way back through the gymnasium, she stopped at
the water fountain...for an extended period of time. She had not
realized how parched she was until the cold water hit the back of
her throat and she could not stop drinking. When she finally backed
away from the fountain, he took a few gulps of water, stopped and
wiped his mouth on his sleeve. Now she was even more amazed.
He had walked all that distance and did not need that much water.

3

Back to the car. She headed for a different hideout. This was a two bedroom apartment on the north side of Frankfurt. She pulled into a parking spot and now he sat there glaring at her with even more suspicion on his face (if that was possible).

She smiled. "It belongs to a friend. I'm watching it for her while she's away."

He did not even look at her. She could tell by his frown that he was not buying her line of nonsense. She had never met anyone (who was not a field agent) who was so suspicious of everything. She got out and headed for the door. He did not move. She went back to the car and opened the door on his side. She stood there with her head cocked to the side and her hands on her hips. He sat there motionless.

"Come on inside…" She leaned forward scowling with her teeth clenched. "…please!"

He gave her that same deadpan look. "Why?"

She sighed in frustration. "So we can both get cleaned up for one thing. We both stink! Don't you want to get cleaned up?"

He clasped his hands across his stomach. "I've got a shower waiting for me back at the barracks. I also have a change of clothing back there as well. What have you got for me…here?"

She gritted her teeth and then calmed herself. She smiled, in an attempt at being congenial. "Come on in and be surprised. You might like it."

He looked at her suspiciously, rolled his eyes and shook his head. He got out of the car slowly. As he followed her to the door, he snorted in disgust several times.

She unlocked the door and in they went. He was totally disinterested in the interior of the small apartment's living room. There was an overstuffed armchair close by, he simply sat down and stared off into space.

"Come on," she ordered. "Get those smelly clothes off so I can clean them."

He looked up at her and frowned. "What am I supposed to wear in the mean time?"

She gave him a seductive grin with one hand on her hip. "Come on and I'll show you."

With his chin on his chest, while shaking his head, he got up and reluctantly followed.

She walked into a combination bathroom/washroom. In here was a sink, a toilet, a bathtub, a washer and a dryer. She opened the lid on the washer and looked back at him. "Well, get your clothes off so I can wash them."

He looked around a little perturbed. "You got a robe...or a towel...or something?"

She gave him a lustful look and licked her lips. "You won't need any of that," she said trying to look as sexy as possible.

He folded his arms and gave her no indication of any form of cooperation. "I think it's about time I got back to the Base."

"What's the matter – are you shy?" Again she tried to look, and sound, as seductive as possible.

"Shy has nothing to do with it. Who are you and what are you really trying to pull off? I want some answers."

She giggled. She pulled her tube top off and threw it into the washer. She pulled her shoes off and then stripped her shorts off. Her shorts followed the tube top. She turned to face him and put her arms behind her back. "Do you really want a robe for what I have in mind?" She was expecting a look of lust and maybe surprise on his face. Instead he still had his arms crossed and was staring right into her eyes...disinterested. Now *she* was totally confused. She was standing there, in front of a young man, completely naked and he was not looking at her body. She tried to push the issue. "Come on, haven't you ever tried to...*sexercise*? *You*...are supposed to lose some weight and hard sex is one of the best ways to do just that."

He remained motionless. His deadpan expression did not change. He still did not look down at her body. He still stared directly into her eyes.

She slowly walked up to him in the most alluring manner she could muster. His gaze and expression did not change. When she got in range, she brought her foot up and kicked him in the side of the head. He never saw it coming and went down to the floor slightly stunned. As he tried to get back up she kicked him in the back of his head, knocking him out completely.

She knelt down, pulled his sweatshirt off and threw it to the side. She rolled him on his back, unbuckled his belt, opened the snap and pulled the zipper down. Then she remembered that his shoes were still on his feet. She shrugged and went to the shoes. The shoes came off and she grimaced from the smell. She threw the shoes over on top of the sweatshirt and then stripped off his socks. She had to do a few adjustments in order to get his pants off, but seeing as how he was unconscious he did not fight her. She got his pants and briefs in one pull…and landed flat on her butt in the process. Each piece of clothing that came off made the smell in the room a little worse than it had been a moment before. She breathed a sigh of relief at having completed the task of undressing him. She emptied the pockets of his pants, gathered all of his clothing up and all of his garments went into the washer. She poured some detergent in and started the machine up.

She let out a deep breath. She went to him and checked to see if there was any sign of him waking up yet. Nothing. She looked him over. He was a decent specimen, albeit overweight, but neck down – far better than neck up. She worked him into a sitting position. She grimaced in disgust as she got him under his arms to drag him to the tub and got that horrible smelling armpit sweat all over her arms. Once she got him next to the tub, she now had to wrestle him into the tub. By the time she finished that task she was covered in sweat herself – both his and hers. She got him into a seated position and started running the water. As the water started coming up, she poured in some bubble bath soap.

He started stirring. She quickly got in the tub, straddled his lap and started rubbing his chest with soapy water. He opened his eyes and then got a startled look on his face when he realized where he was and what she was doing. He looked in her eyes and then down at her breasts. 'Finally,' she thought. 'Some form of masculine lust. He is human.' His gaze, almost immediately, went back up to her eyes.

"What's going on?" He sat there with a little fear in his eyes now. "How did I get in here?" He started to push her away, however, there was no spot to "properly" place his hands.

She smiled. "I helped you in here. I told you that we both needed to bathe. So here we are." She gave him another lustful smile.

"You said a shower. This ain't no shower." He tried to get up.

She put her hands on his shoulders. "Stay where you are," she said still smiling. "This is even better. We can wash each other." She giggled as she started rubbing his neck.

He grabbed her wrists and tried to push her away. "No! No more of this crap until you explain what is really going on here."

She pushed herself onto him. "You're right. I have been holding back." She relaxed. "Look we both stink. As soon as we finish cleaning each other, I'll give you a full explanation."

"I'll clean myself," he growled. "You keep your hands to yourself."

She cupped her breasts and shook them a little. "Are you sure you don't want to clean me?"

Again that angry stare directly into her eyes.

She sat back a little disgusted and backed away towards the

spigot. She rubbed herself down while he cleaned himself, still with that angry glare.

He snarled at her again. "How did I get in the bathtub... naked?"

"After you went to sleep, I undressed you and put you in here," she said bluntly. "You obviously were more tired than you thought after that long walk."

His eyebrows went up. "Sleep? Hah! I saw how you handled that idiot at the Rec Center. The side of my head hurts. Was the sleeping pill your fist or foot?"

She started shampooing her hair. "My foot." She giggled. "Once on the side of your head and the other to your back. Then you went beddy-by-boo. I couldn't get you to cooperate one way... so...I had to get some cooperation in another way."

"Something is going on here and it's aimed right between my eyes. You had better give me some kind of good explanation or else I'm going to expose you...uh..." He looked off to the side confused.

"To whom? You haven't figured out what's going on, so what or who are you going to expose me to?"

He growled and splashed some soapy water through his hair.

She finished washing her hair and dunked her head under the water to get all of the soap out. She then stood up, exposing herself completely, trying to see if she could get any reaction out of him. All that happened was a quick glance at her pubic region and then he quickly glanced away. Not much, but it helped for the moment. 'He is a man, he is just upset because he's not in control of the situation,' she thought.

She stepped out of the tub and grabbed a towel. She wrapped her hair in it and headed out of the bathroom. She went into the hallway and took a quick glance at the front door. There was a large manila envelope, a duffel bag and two large boxes that had been placed inside the door, while the bath was going on. She smiled in satisfaction.

She went back to the tub. "Are you ready to get out yet?"

"You seem to have the only towel...wrapped around your head."

She wrinkled her lips then giggled. She put her hands on her hips. "Do you really need a towel?"

"Yes," he spat.

She smiled. "Remember, I undressed you. You've got nothing to be ashamed of."

Again he stared directly into her eyes with that angry glare. He crossed his arms and turned to stare at the wall. She was amazed at his self control.

She gave up and went to the linen closet for a bath towel. She placed it on the floor beside the tub and walked away, doing everything she could do hide any disappointment on her face.

The washing machine was finished now, so she moved the clothing to the dryer. She then went into the bedroom and dried herself off. She left the towel in the bedroom.

She went back to the front door and picked up the envelope. She checked to make sure that the curtains were closed. She did not need to give a nudie show to the entire neighborhood. German men were already too oversexed and she did not need them knocking on her door. She sat down on the couch, opened the envelope and started thumbing through the paperwork.

He came out of the bathroom with that angry glare still on his face. "Where'd you hide my clothing?"

She gave him her best smile. "It is all in the dryer, with my clothes."

"If you don't start explaining something, real quick, as soon as my clothes are done, I'm dressed and out of here."

She patted a place on the couch next to her. "Sit down and I'll explain."

"Would you mind covering up?"

She gave him a pouting look. "Don't you like what you see?"

"No! You're not my wife, so unless you're a whore, you should put some clothes on in the presence of strangers." He walked over and sat down in the armchair.

She got up from the couch, walked over to him and sat down next to him on the arm of the chair. She handed him one of the documents she had pulled out of the envelope. She leaned back a little to watch his reaction.

He looked at it angrily. His expression changed to confusion. "What...? How...? Where did you get this...? What's going on?"

She shrugged. "What does it look like?"

"It looks...like a...marriage certificate. It...but...what?! How?!"

She put an arm on his shoulder. "According to this, darling, we have been married for almost three years. We got married when you were stationed at Shaw AFB in South Carolina. You remember Shaw, don't you?"

"Who is this clown that signed it? Who is Chaplain... Samuel Bates?"

She snickered. "Colonel Bates is the military chaplain who married us, darling."

"Well I didn't sign it."

"Really darling? Look at the groom signature block."

"Okay I see...HOW DID YOU DO THAT?" He jumped up and glared at her.

She could see the rage in his eyes, however, she was not really concerned. "We need to be married for this mission."

"Well...I want a divorce...NOW! Besides that, you have nothing to back what you're saying and...I'm going to find my way back to the Base...and..." His expression changed to a look of dull normal confusion. "Mission?"

She laughed. "There's nothing back at the Base for you right now. Take a look at the front door."

He looked in the direction of the door. He saw the duffel bag and the two boxes. He saw his name stenciled on them. "That's my…uh…what's in the boxes?"

"I imagine that your clothing is in the duffel bag and your… other things are in the boxes." She stood up and put her arms around him. "All of your possessions have been packed up and you don't even have a room anymore. This is your home, darling…until I say otherwise."

"I'm leaving," he growled. He headed for the door. He was going to get some clothing out, put it on and depart. He woke up laying in front of the couch. He had a new pain in the back of his head. He looked up at her and scowled.

She was standing over him, still naked. She was looking down at him – still naked – shaking her head. "You need to calm down, darling. You seem to pass out each time you get upset."

He looked up at her with nothing but hatred. "If, I repeat IF we were married, then there would be a wedding…" He noticed the ring finger on his left hand. He glared at her again. His entire body went limp and he closed his eyes. "Where did that stinkin' thing come from?"

When he opened his eyes she smiled and showed him the rings on her left hand. "Any more questions…darling?"

"There's a lot more stuff you haven't taken care of," he snarled.

She sat down on him, straddling his waist. With a contented smile she started pulling things out of the big envelope. "Let's see. We've already seen the marriage certificate. Now, what else? Oh, I have a dependent ID card that shows that you're my husband. I have our passports."

"Our...WHAT?"

"Right here, darling."

"How did you get hold of my passport?"

"Like I told you, darling, we need to pass off as married for this mission."

"Where did you get all of this crap? Wait a minute - my duty section is expecting me to be at work tomorrow - at 6AM."

She pulled out another document. "This is your orders, saying that you're temporarily assigned...elsewhere...indefinitely." She leaned down closer to his face. "Darling," she said forcefully.

He grabbed the orders and looked at them closely. He looked at her with desperation on his face. "What're you doin' to me?"

"I'm trying to tell you, that at the moment, you are my husband, until this mission is over."

He went limp again. "I want a divorce," he said bluntly.

"Not until the mission is over."

"I want a divorce," he said more forcefully.

"I'm going to give you a full briefing later on."

"I want a divorce," he reiterated.

"Right now, all you need to know is that we need to get used to each other."

"I don't want to get used to you. I want a divorce," he said with more force.

"You'll get one later. You have all the instructions that apply for now."

"I...want...a...divorce...now," he said in a sinister manner.

"Stop saying that."

"I want a divorce," he barked louder.

"You're not going to get anything until this mission is over."

"I want a divorce."

She lost her patience. She punched him in the lower abdomen. "You need to start listening and quit being a jerk."

He wheezed and grimaced from the pain. "Who's the jerk... JERK?!"

"YOU, jerk. Now, are you ready to start listening?" she said sarcastically.

"I want a divorce," he wheezed.

She punched him in the lower abdomen again. "I can keep this up longer than you can, darling," she snarled through her teeth.

He growled in pain.

She stood up. She reached down to help him up. "Come on, darling," she said smiling again.

He snarled at her through his wheezing and flopped down on the couch.

She pulled him up and led him to the bedroom. He fell onto

the bed still having problems breathing. She pushed him over onto his back and crawled in bed on top of him. "As I said, the first part is that we have to get used to each other. So, darling, let's have some fun here in the bed."

He reached up and grabbed hold of her midsection from the sides and threw her completely off of the bed.

She responded with another lightning kick to the head.

He woke up with a new headache on the left side of his head...and he was handcuffed to the bed – with fur-lined bracelets. He was having a little problem opening his left eye. He looked up and saw his hands were in cuffs hooked to the brass poles at the head of the bed.

She was sitting on his stomach again with that stupid smile on her face.

He groaned in frustration and tried pulling at the cuffs.

"Are you ready to start cooperating, darling?"

"I hate you," he snarled.

"No you don't, darling. We are having a few problems in our marriage and we have to get away for a while. Okay, darling?"

"Stop calling me that," he moaned.

"Well, what do you want me to call you?"

"A complete stranger," he gave her that continuous scowl.

"You'd better come up with some kind of term of endearment, or else, Bub!"

He looked up with a childish grin. "How about...
hemorrhoid?"

She slapped his face. "Try again, darling," she said
impatiently.

"Okay, total pain in the..."

She slapped him harder. "Not good."

"Why are you doing this to me?" he whined.

"Because I need you for a few weeks."

"No you don't," he countered.

She smiled. "Hey, baby, the sooner you cooperate, the
sooner the suffering will be over and you will be able to get back to
your loser lifestyle."

He groaned. "What do you want?"

"I want you to cooperate. Work with me."

He glared at her. "And...that involves...having sex...with...
YOU?"

"We need to put up the façade that we *are* married."

He smiled again. "Okay! Good! Let's start arguing!"

She slapped him harder across the face. "Right now, all we
need to do is get used to each other's touch." She laid down lower
on him.

"You don't turn me on," he said churlishly.

She sat back up and snarled at him. "What is your problem?

I've come across guys that I had to kick the snot out of them...in order to keep them off of me. I can't get you to say or do anything nice. What's the matter with you?"

He grabbed two of the brass poles at the head of the bed. His face was showing nothing but rage. "Women have never done *anything* good to or for me! That includes my four sisters and my mother. They all treat me like crap! Every time a woman says she is going to do something nice to or for me, is always ends up as a lie or a dirty trick of some kind. That's the way it has been all of my life! I don't see or hear anything that says you're going to do anything different."

"Didn't your father have anything to do with the attitude of your mother and sisters?"

"He died when I was two years old. All I had was four older sisters and that cranky piece of crap that was my mother, who told me, every day, how evil I was because of those things hanging between my legs. I joined the military to get away from her and those wretched sisters. I haven't written to any of them since I put the uniform on...and I don't intend to. I've broken off all communication with all of them...permanently! No woman has ever done anything, ANYTHING, nice for me. All I hear, coming out of your vomit-hole, is that you're planning on using me and then when you're finished, I'm yesterday's newspaper."

'How did he know that I'm going to...dump him?' she thought. 'Maybe I did pick the wrong one.' "Look, I understand what you're saying but your name is on all of the paperwork and it's all dated today. Your Commanding Officer has been informed that you are temporarily somewhere else – indefinitely. You're mine for a while. Get used to it – for a while. After this is over…you'll never see me again." She thought for a moment. 'Because you'll probably be in a Russian Gulag.'

He went totally limp and just lay there staring off into space. "Yesterday's newspaper," he muttered.

She hoped that he was ready to cooperate. She reached down and started trying to stimulate him. He felt her playing with his genitals. He started trying to avoid an erection by thinking of mathematical equations or something unrelated to sex or anything erotic. She was persistent and knew what she was doing.

'$1 + 1 = 2, 1 + 2 = 3, 1 + 3 = $ *Oh my god*! $2 + 4 = 7$…or 10 or…something. *No*! $1 + 1 = 2, 2 + 2 = 4$ $3 +$ *oh stop that*!' He was quickly losing the battle.

She gave him a loving smile. "Do you like that feeling, honey? We're just getting started. I can do…things for you that will send you to heaven."

"I've heard the same thing from the whores on Weiss Strasse," he pointed out. "You don't seem to be any different."

"You have to pay them…and there's no sincerity."

"Guess again, you dumb broad. A whore is the most honest woman on the face of the earth. You know what you're getting and there's no guesswork. You get what you pay for and you can't expect anything else unless you pay her more."

"I've heard that they all say that they're clean. Then you find out that they were fibbing when you start dripping. Is that really what you call honesty?"

"That's why I wear a rubber. That helps keep them honest. What kind of a rubber do I have to keep you honest? What do I have from you that in any way, shape or form says that you've told me anything that I can believe?"

He forgot about his mental diversions. She now had raised him to full arousal and she sat down on him achieving full penetration. He now was trying to think of a way to stop ejaculation. 'Distract your mind, distract your mind, distract your mind, something, something, something, something, anything, anything, something.'

He was getting desperate. He had never been able to trust any woman. His four sisters and mother had put him through all kinds of torture when he was growing up. They treated him like garbage while telling him that he (and all other men) was treating them like garbage. After his father's death there were very few men in his life that could give him anything positive about being a man. Three of his sisters had married, before he left home (permanently) and all three had been divorced quickly. They drove their husbands crazy and then blamed the men for the problems. Now, here is a woman who is trying to get him to do…what?

She kept pumping. The look on his face was a puzzlement. Was he enjoying it or trying to figure out a way of fighting it. She started worrying about whether or not all of the bruises she was leaving on him would hurt the mission. Her legs were getting a little tired from the constant motion. He had been moving his head back and forth with a look of aggravation and desperation. He suddenly arched his back, held his breath momentarily and then went limp while breathing hard. She relaxed, laying on top of him and panting a little.

She raised back up with a satisfied smile on her face. "Now you know. I can turn you on, get you off and knock you out. Now, are you ready to talk turkey about the mission?"

He clenched his teeth. "What do you want?"

She breathed a sigh of relief. "In a couple of weeks, we are going to take a trip. Before we go, we have to get used to each other. No problems with touching and we have to know a few things about each other. This way we will appear to be a normal married couple. Ya got that?"

"Where are we supposed to go?"

"You'll find out later."

"I'm not liking this at all! You only tell me what you want. If I try to find out something else, as to what or why, all of a sudden you clam up, change the subject or knock me out. This whole thing SUCKS!"

"You'll find out what you need to know, when you need to know it."

He grunted. "Typical."

She got a little upset with that remark. "What do you mean by that?"

He narrowed his eyes and gave her a phony grin. "You don't have the need to know," he said in a mocking manner.

She felt like punching him again. One thing she could not stand was someone using her words against her. "Well, honey, we're going to get used to each other and you'll find out that I have the need to know and then you'll tell me."

"You first!" he grunted.

"Me first...what?"

"Start telling me what's going on."

She leaned closer to him. "I am in charge," she said angrily. "I decide who needs to know what, when – got that?"

He huffed. "Yeah! Typical female utopianist. Now get off of me!"

She responded lackadaisically. "Any particular reason why?"

"My 'thing' is still inside you and I gotta take a wicked piss. So unless you want your 'goody hole' to turn into a urinal, you'll get off of me and get rid of these shackles."

She was totally surprised by that. It was irritating because he was right. She could not do anything but cooperate with his... bodily need. She stared at him stupidly for a moment then jumped off. She got the keys off of the nightstand and unshackled him.

He snarled at her as he got up. He headed out the only door to the room and checked other rooms in the short hallway. He walked into the bathroom to the toilet, lifted the lid and relieved himself.

She came up behind him and put her arms around his waist. She felt him tense up as she rubbed his stomach. "That's what I'm talking about. You freak when I touch you. We need to accept each other's touch without any problems of any type," she cooed lovingly.

"That's gonna take a *lot* of time. I can't stand *any* of your touches…at all."

"So let's start. We're both all sweaty again. Let's take another bath," she said on a cheery note.

He let out his breath as a growl instead of a sigh. "I want to get your stuff off of me. If you're in the bathtub as well, I can't get your sweat off of me without something else ending up on me."

She giggled playfully. "What are you complaining about? I've got something of you up inside me. I have to do a lot more than just soap my sexy little body off."

"You're almost as sexy as a five day dead aardvark," he muttered.

She slapped his right hip as hard as she could. "That attitude is going to go as well. As I said, we have to be used to each other."

"Well if I'm going to be banging you – does getting you pregnant enter into your super-secret plan of total idiocy?"

"Don't worry, I'm on the pill."

"Well what happens if you *do* get pregnant?"

She grabbed hold of his hair and yanked his head back. "It's not your problem or concern," she said angrily. "I'm not going to allow any pregnancy, especially with you. Now, I don't hear any more stuff hitting the water in the toilet, so let's get in the tub and wash each other off."

He raised his right hip and let fly with a barnyard noise that left a certain "air" hanging around the bathroom. She groaned and climbed into the tub while holding her nose.

4

They had been locked in the apartment for three days. She was still having problems connecting and getting him to cooperate. Parading around nude was not getting the results that she was expecting either. She had always had to push men away. Any man that had not been interested had usually been rather effeminate and in all probability a homosexual. She just did not know how to categorize this one. They had copulated only once since the original session and she had definitely had to force that one as well.

They were laying next to each other in bed. He was showing his usual lack of interest. She huffed in frustration. "What's your problem? What is it that you don't like about me?"

He blew a raspberry out into the air and stared at the ceiling blankly. "You snatch me out of my nice, normal life. You make a silly claim that we are married, with bogus paperwork to back it up. You won't tell me what is going on with this whole idiotic super-secret bogus affair, but I'm supposed to go along with it, without question. I'm practically a prisoner in this little whorehouse hideout of yours. What could possibly be the problem? Oh…I don't know. Maybe it's the fact that I'm being treated like a mushroom."

"What? A mushroom? What do you mean by that?"

"Mushrooms thrive on bull crap and being kept in the dark."

She had a hard time stifling her laughter. "I'll tell you what: If you cooperate with me, I'll give you some more information. I don't like keeping people in the dark, but sometimes I don't have a choice. So, cooperate a little more and I'll give you more of what you want." She gave him a friendly smile.

He scoffed. "You want me to plug you, and you call that cooperation?"

She sighed. "The whole thing is based on the two of us acting totally like a married couple. Married people don't flinch away from each other's touch. There is no problem with touch. That is what we need to be like. I need to know your little idiosyncrasies and you need to know mine. That way there will be no flinching. In order to do that, I'm telling you that I'm going to cooperate with whatever you do sexually. Just be yourself and let me be myself. You can do anything you want to do. Does that help any?"

"So…I can do whatever is normal…for me?"

"Yes."

"Whatever is normal…between husband and wife?"

"Yes."

He lifted his legs, spread them slightly and blasted a horrendous fart. He looked at her and smiled. "Isn't that what men normally do in bed?"

She gritted her teeth and gave him a strained smile. "That's not really…what I had in mind." She turned away to get away from the smell. He had eaten a lot of beans lately and now she knew why. She wondered how long he had been holding all that atrocious pressure back. Nice move: Sucker her into enticing it out. She could hardly wait to use him as a decoy and dump him in a really bad situation.

She waited for the smell to subside. Trying to unclench her jaws she snuggled closer to him. "Okay, that's normal for you." She gave him a hard shot to a very soft spot that was meant to cause a lot of pain. He doubled up in pain. "That...will be my normal reaction to that act of yours."

He muttered a few curses under his breath.

"If you cooperate with me, I will give you some more information. You want more information but you won't cooperate with me."

"Why won't you give me all of the information?" he asked with a definite strain through the pain.

"Your security clearance is not high enough to give you all of the info. What would happen if I gave it to you and you leak it?"

He scoffed angrily. "You've kept me locked in this whorehouse prison. I have no one to talk with except you. You don't even have a goldfish. Who would I leak the information to?"

"Not the point. You don't communicate with anyone until I say so. You weren't chosen at random. We used a very sophisticated computer program to choose you. Does that help a little bit?"

"No it does NOT! What was fed into a computer...that picks me...to just hole up in this apartment, diddling you...and being kept in the dark about anything else?"

She sighed. "What's your security clearance?"

"You know very well," he spat. "SECRET!"

"So I can't give you any more information at this time."

"So why should I cooperate with you at all? Speaking of that, what gives you the authority to use torture to get me to cooperate?"

"That's classified," she countered.

He growled.

They both stared at the ceiling in silence.

She woke up with a start. She had fallen asleep from the boredom of waiting for him to do something. Somehow he had crawled up on top of her, penetrated her and was pumping away. She had been trying to get him to have sex with her, however she had hoped to be awake when it started. He had initiated the act and that was what she had been pushing for, but not quite in this way. What disturbed her was that he had been able to do all that without waking her up. She was usually a very light sleeper, so she could not understand how he had done the deed so covertly.

Maybe her training was failing her. Her last assignment had ended badly with another man who was very oversexed. He was a Spaniard who she was supposed to contact and learn everything that she could about him and his underground operations. It turned out that he was telling tall tales, just to get women in bed with him, by fair means or foul. He would leave the impression that he was some kind of mobster or spy and if a woman tried to stop him or press charges against him, she and her entire family would suffer the ultimate penalty. She had seen through his pile of nonsense and was ready to break it off completely, sending a full report of what kind of a phony he was...until he drugged her and she woke up chained to a bed, with him having all the fun he wanted. After he let her loose, she had left him, with a broken neck, face down, in a river near Madrid.

The sex with Bradley was a start in getting her plan moving. He was doing what she wanted albeit somewhat on his terms. It was a start. She lay there, giving no objection or hindrance. She did everything she could to act as if she was enjoying it.

When he finished he rolled off of her and lay there panting for a few moments before falling asleep. She propped herself up on her elbows and stared at him. She shook her head and sighed. She glanced over at the clock. It showed 12:19AM. She shrugged, yawned, put her head back on her pillow and closed her eyes.

She woke up again startled. He was on top of her again. Again he had crawled up on her and penetrated her without waking her. This was becoming bothersome. After he was finished he rolled off of her and was back asleep again quickly. She looked over at the clock. It was just after 3AM.

She sat up and tried to figure out why she had not awakened as soon as he started each session. Her training seemed to be totally nonoperational. One: She should have awakened once he got close enough to touch, any place on her body. Two: She should have awakened swinging. Any surprise wakeup, she had been trained to beat someone bloody and ask questions later. Maybe it was the situation. She was trying to get used to him...maybe she had...she hoped.

There were four more nights of the repetitious sex acts. Each time she became even more disturbed at how she was not waking up until he was well into it.

She woke up in pain. She was on her stomach and he was on top of her pumping away.

"What…are…you…doing?" she screamed.

"What…you…wanted…me to…do," he grunted.

"I said…I wanted…you to…have sex…with me."

"Yeah…that's what…I'm doing."

"That's…NOT my…va…gina…you…idiot!"

"And?"

"And, what? What…are you…doing?"

He stopped pumping and lay there panting. "Don't married couples experiment with different types and positions?"

She squawked in exasperation. Again he was doing what she wanted in a sideways manner and using her words against her. She clenched her teeth and just accepted the act…while he was doing it. He had her pinned down and she could not figure out any way to get the proper leverage to punch, or kick, the snot out of him. He was in complete control.

He rolled off of her. He looked at her with a smirk on his face. "I always wondered what that would be like. You told me that we should act like a normal married couple – okay, I did. Are you going to tell me that you never wondered what it would be like…to do it that way?"

She propped herself up on her elbows and glared at him. "Okay! Yes, I *have* wondered," she said angrily. "Now, I don't have to wonder any more! Now...I know that I DON'T like it." She leaned closer and spoke menacingly. "Don't you EVER...do that again."

She got up out of bed and staggered awkwardly to the bathroom. She sat down on the toilet and liberally smeared her aching anus with hemorrhoid cream. She got up, walked to the sink and washed her hands...several times. She opened the medicine cabinet, pulled out the aspirin and threw three of them into her mouth and swallowed. She looked at her reflection in the mirror and did everything she could to calm down.

She headed back to the bedroom. He was in the hallway looking rather smug.

"Are you *sure*...you don't want to try that again?" he asked merrily.

Her answer was a right jab and a left cross. She would have kicked him, however, her legs would not cooperate with a move like that right now. He hit the floor and did not move. She looked down at him with her own smug grin. She waddled back to the bed and crawled in trying to not think about how much it had hurt and how humiliating it had been. She had a difficult time trying to find a good position to sleep in.

She woke up with the sun shining through a gap I the curtains. She looked over at his side of the bed – he was not there. She got out of bed, feeling a little better...but not much. She peered into the hallway. He was not there either. She went into the living room. He was asleep on the couch.

She sighed, walked over to the couch and shook him. "Wake up! We need to talk."

He turned over and she saw the bruises on his face. He glared at her, stood up and headed for the bathroom without saying a thing.

She followed him into the bathroom. "Hey, Brad, we need to talk."

He turned his back to her as he urinated. He said nothing.

She came up behind him and put her arms around him, trying to be nice. He let go of his penis, spraying the whole toilet and pushed her arms away. After pushing her away, he grabbed his penis and aimed it back into the toilet.

"We need to talk," she said through clenched teeth.

"The only time you talk, I end up with a new bruise. Go away!"

"I'm trying to get your attention," she spat back.

He finished what he was doing and walked away. She looked down at the toilet and around the room in disgust. "Hey! Are you gonna clean up this mess and flush the thing?"

He stopped and turned back to her. "This is your apartment, not mine. If you want it cleaned up – you can clean it. I *didn't* ask to be here, so I don't care what it looks like…or *smells* like." He turned away and stomped back to the couch.

She followed him with a feeling that she really wanted to

belt him again. "What am I supposed to do when you treat me like trash? You have not shown me one ounce of respect since I first met you."

He rolled his eyes and stared upwards with his mouth open while shaking his head. He glared back at her disillusioned. "How much respect have you shown me? You've knocked me out five or six times. You won't answer ANY of my questions. You want everything according to *your* wants or needs without one iota of caring or respecting *my* wants or needs. As I said – you treat me like a mushroom! Well guess what, you phony wifey-poo – respect is a two way street. If you refuse to show me any respect, then take a good guess at what you're going to get back in your DISRESPECTFUL face!"

She hung her head and her shoulders sagged. She took several deep breaths to calm herself and think. She looked up and saw that he was now sitting there with his arms folded and a very angry scowl on his face. She quietly walked to the couch and sat down...and nearly yelped in pain. She gasped and grimaced as she changed her position to where she was sitting on one hip. The pain from his shenanigan was still there. "Okay, okay," she sighed. "The people that I work with are looking for an individual. The type of person he is, is what makes our little diversion necessary."

He looked at her as if she were insane. He scoffed, rolled his eyes and looked away.

"We're supposed to go where he is and...just be seen... publicly. It will be leaked, before we get there, that we're looking for him. While he's wasting resources following us, there will be other agents following him. They'll blend in better with the surrounding community, so he should not notice them – just us."

He looked at her is disbelief with his eyebrows raised. "Agents? Diversion?"

She grunted in pain as she tried to get into a more comfortable position. "Yes, a diversion. We won't be doing anything that would give the slightest appearance of looking for or at him."

He closed his eyes and moved his lips silently as if he were going over what she had just said. "Why do you need *me* to do this? Don't you…AGENTS…have some special people who are trained in this…sort of thing?"

"They *are* professionals! You are *not*! He would recognize them…by their actions. I'm depending on that – the fact that he will *not* recognize *you*."

He scoffed. "WHAT?"

She had to reposition again. "Look, we've been trying to get a line on this guy for years. He keeps on giving us the slip. He also seems to have a good idea of who all of us are. We need a face that he doesn't recognize. That can give us a chance to keep him in one place, long enough to find out more about him, his network and his habits."

"New face?"

"He has some kind of network of people, all over the continent. Somehow, they're able to slip him past us, as well as themselves. He somehow has a good idea of who each one of us is. If he sees a new face, and has no clue where you came from or who you are…he will have to admonish someone and then try to find out...just exactly who you are and where you fit in. Meanwhile, as he's looking at us, our people can covertly watch and see who he contacts...and where. That will give us some leads to who he works with."

"So...if I'm some kind of bait...why don't I get a phony name and identification?"

"If he finds out your name – from your passport or whatever – and he sees you with me, he will think that Bradley Dooley *is* a phony. He will then try to find out who you *really* are."

"So if this is some kind of secret agent stuff, won't he try to kill me?"

She gave up trying to find a comfortable sitting position and stood up. "We're not a bunch of murderous movie secret agents. Killing an enemy agent only happens if it helps the mission...and it rarely does...unless you're defending your own life. The problem with killing someone is that that person will be replaced. If you already know that someone is an agent and you know where they are, you know where to look and who to look for...when you go into a certain area. If you eliminate someone – now you have to start from scratch, investigating and trying to find out just exactly who the replacement is. That's time consuming and can be a royal headache if you get a false lead and start following the wrong person."

He grunted in disgust. "So that's what I am...a false lead. You want this...*person*...to start looking at me and...trying to waste his time figuring out...who I am."

"That's basically it," she said as she shrugged.

His now looked even more disgusted. He shook his head and closed his eyes. "Did it *kill* you to say that?"

She looked down and started twiddling her thumbs. "No," she said sheepishly.

"So…why couldn't you tell me that from the beginning?"

She looked up. "I was told that I shouldn't tell you," she said in a guilty manner.

He looked down. "This is ridiculous." He sat motionless for a few moments. "All right, tell me how I got chosen for this stupid puppet job. Why couldn't you have picked someone else?"

She snickered. "You weren't the first choice."

He looked at her with a blank stare.

"The first choice was rear-ended by a drunk driver. He's in a coma. The second choice…he turned out to be a total buffoon. He punched out his Division Commander *and* the Division Sergeant Major."

"Sergeant Major? That's an Army rank! What're you doing with me?"

"I work with any branch of the US Military."

He contemplated for a few moments, shrugged and grudgingly accepted it.

"The third choice went Absent Without Leave. The fourth somehow ended in in a 'non-available' status. They never told me why they axed the fifth or sixth choice. They just told me to go with you."

He stared at her for a few moments. "So where are we supposed to go...to parade around in front of this yo-yo?"

"I don't know."

He threw his hands up. "Oh come on! You were doing so well!"

"I *really* don't know," she spat back at him. "One report puts him in southern Italy. Other report puts him in eastern Austria. Another report puts him in the French Riviera. Another one puts him in Bremerhaven. The last one we got puts him in Rotterdam. Shall I go on? We're supposed to be getting used to each other while they confirm which of the reports is accurate. Until then...we're in limbo, waiting for a firm destination."

He sighed while frowning at her. "So this yahoo gets around."

"Quite a bit."

"Again, did it kill you to tell me that?"

She smoothed her hair back and sighed. "I was just following orders. If you were deemed not ready, they would have chosen someone else...to be my quarrelsome husband."

He tilted his head back. "Who is supposed to make that decision?"

"It'll be partially mine and partially the guy who...married us."

He gave her a sideways glance and she gave him a helpless shrug.

He made a loud sound as he blew air out. "You say that… *he*…will be observing us. How much of the time do you think *he* will be watching us, once we're there, wherever *there* is?"

"We have to treat it as if we're under scrutiny 24 hours a day. He might get some listening devices in the hotel room. He might have one of his people acting as our waiter in a restaurant. We are the diversion and we have to act like we don't care about him. That's what the other people are going to be doing."

He groaned. "Are you saying that…we might have to put on some…porno peep show for this…pervert creep?"

She gave him a hapless smile and nodded. "We are married… and we have to act like it. That should throw him off even further."

He covered his face with his hands. He dropped his hands and looked up at her confused. "Don't you have a problem with that?"

"If that's what the mission calls for," she shrugged, "what can I say?"

He shook his head helplessly. "What if I had been infected… with VD?"

"Then both of us would be going to the hospital for a *silver bullet*," she said bluntly. "Once we were cured…we'd still be doing the mission."

He hung his head and sighed. "And all that *crap* was supposed to be kept super-secret from me."

"Unfortunately…yes."

He looked up at her and smiled. "I still don't believe a word that you're saying."

She stammered a moment and then grunted in anger. "Why?"

"You're a woman, you're breathing and you're awake. That means - you're telling me a whopper of a lie just to get what *you* want. You're going to use me and then throw me away." He sighed. "You women are all the same. Always have been...always will be."

"If what I'm saying was a fabrication...that would be illegal."

He cleared his throat. "Sure," he said in a demeaning manner.

She huffed at him. 'How does he know what I'm going to do to him?' she thought. 'I can hardly wait...to dump you...you... prop jockey.'

In spite of their differences, the next few days went a lot smoother. They discussed several areas about each other: Likes/ dislikes, allergies, relatives, a story on how they met, why they married and what the cover story of marital problems was going to be.

She learned a lot about his four older sisters and was starting to understand why he hated women, in general, so much. She guessed that if she had been treated that badly, she would be rather sensitive and hateful as well. If even one fourth of his horror stories were true, she could not really blame him for his attitude.

They went out a few times on actual romantic dates, so they would have some kind of history of dating. Each time they went on a date, he would look around the restaurant or bar they were in for any familiar faces. For some reason she always picked an establishment where no one seemed to be able to speak English and he found out that she spoke fluent German (big surprise). He wondered how many other languages this secretive headache spoke.

They discussed the places that he had frequented in South Carolina. There was also a phony concoction she gave him that she was from a place called Raphine, Virginia.

She finally decided that her "Class A" sucker was ready. The only problem that she saw was going to be breaking the news as to exactly where they were going…especially since it was snowing most of the time…and where they were going, it was usually a very cold winter.

5

They packed their clothing in suitcases, other than the military duffel bag. That could have been a problem. He did not question the fact that she had him pack a lot of winter clothing. It was getting into winter here and she had told him that the "mark" was not in any warm area...at this time.

The morning before they headed to the Frankfurt airport, she told him that she was going to replace all of his military identification with civilian documentation. She gave him a new phony Georgia driver's license. She replaced all of her ID material with equally phony stuff that coincided with his documentation.

She told him that they would find out where they were going once they got to the airport. It could be anywhere so...he should not be too surprised.

They got to the airport. She went to a phone booth and made a call. She came back to him with a helpless smile on her face. "Before this started, he was seen in Yugoslavia. Shortly after that he was spotted in Naples. We figured that he'd stay on this side of the iron curtain...for a while."

He looked at her with a little fear in his eyes. He looked off shaking his head. "Yugoslavia? Great!"

She looked around in an uncertain manner. "Our tickets are in a locker."

He looked at her suspiciously. "What for?"

"Again, we might be under scrutiny here. If they see me contacting someone, then they'll start following that individual as well."

He grunted. "Which locker?"

She pulled a key out of her pocket and showed him the number. "This one."

He looked at the key in a rather befuddled and concerned manner. 'Where did that key come from?' he thought. 'If she's got to stay away from any contact...where...?'

They found the locker and pulled the tickets out.

"The airline tells us where we're going," she said as she opened the envelope. She handed him his ticket.

He frowned. "What airline is this?" He looked at it as if he had never seen a ticket in his life. "I don't recognize it."

She bit her lip and closed her eyes. "That...Russian airline: Aeroflot. That usually means that...we're going somewhere...on the other side of the iron curtain."

He looked at her with hate and horror. She smiled helplessly and tried to calm him. He looked back and forth several times at the ticket and at her. His expression never changed.

"The other side," he snarled. "GREAT! Just the place that I've *never* wanted to see."

After that he said nothing. He just glared at her as the baggage was tagged and put on the conveyer belt.

She gave him a bit of a guilty look. "You remember that

we're having a few marital problems. From the look on your face, I don't think we'll have too many difficulties in proving that particular problem exists."

He just glared – whenever he did look at her.

They headed for the gate and he still said nothing to her. When their flight was called, he was still silent. They got on the plane and still he remained silent. His teeth were clenched so tight that she thought he was going to break a few teeth. The plane pulled away from the gate – still nothing from him. The plane taxied to the runway and took off. He sat there staring forward.

The only reaction that she saw was when he was offered the in-flight meal. He simply shook his head. He did not ask for anything to drink. He just sat there glaring off into the distance like a crazed zombie.

The plane landed and he still said nothing. When they deplaned, he just walked along silently to claim their baggage. He still just stood there and glared while she pulled the baggage off the line.

They went to customs. They were scrutinized by five men as two others looked through their baggage - thoroughly.

When asked whether they were there for business or pleasure, she fed them the "story" that had been concocted. They were a married couple who were having problems. They came to a place that they knew very little about, they did not know the language and they did not know anyone in the area, so the only ones that they had to communicate with was each other. They were not planning on going on any tour. They were just going to be with each other in order to attempt to get closer and patch up their relationship.

He stood there and nodded each time she said something and did not in any way dispute her words. He looked at the faces of the men behind the customs agents and figured, in his mind, that none of them were buying the line of garbage that she was spreading all over. He figured that the stuff that was coming out of her mouth would have fertilized every crop of wheat, barley, rye, turnips and corn in Kansas, Missouri, Nebraska, Oklahoma, Texas, Arkansas and Iowa combined. He had gone over it several times with her and he now found it hard to buy as well.

They were given a list of rules that they had to adhere to while in Russia. As they left the customs area he read the list silently. A few times he shook he head and scoffed. He had no intention of reading it out loud because he figured that she already knew everything that was written in this pamphlet.

They changed their Deutsche Marks for some local Russian Rubles and were told that they could not take any Russian money out of the country. When they got ready to leave, all the Russian money would have to be exchanged for some other currency.

She found a taxi driver, who understood English, and headed for their hotel.

Still Bradley was tight jawed. He continued his silence. He looked around as they rode to the hotel but made no comments.

They arrived at the hotel and went to check in. They were again scrutinized by someone in the background as someone else did the paperwork.

He was not sure who the man in the background was. Bradley decided to start a staring contest with the blonde stranger who had a somewhat scraggly handlebar moustache. The blonde man was unperturbed and stared back with a blank look on his face. The two of them continued that staring until it was time for Bradley and Marie to head for their room.

Staring at the Russian had seemed the thing to do because there was nothing else to look at. The walls of the hotel were covered in a flowery wall paper that appeared to be in a condition where it predated the Russian revolution. Maybe the Tsar Nicholas had told them not to change anything until he got back – and they had adhered to the request.

They went up to the room and after getting rid of a very boring bellhop they both fell on the bed and stared at the ceiling.

She turned to him apprehensively. "Well, what do you think of this place so far?"

He scoffed. "It needs another shade of gray. I wonder if they know that there *are* other colors. That wallpaper...is so old, all of the flowers have changed to gray as well."

She breathed a sigh of relief. 'He can talk,' she thought. "From what I understand, there are some real colorful buildings in the area. The Kremlin is supposed to be quite a sight."

He sat up. "I thought we were here for each other, not some sight-seeing tour. There isn't much about Russia that I'm really interested in."

She giggled. "Okay, so let's get interested in each other."

She crawled on top of him and started kissing him.

He responded by pushing her sweatshirt up and unhooked her bra. He was a little disgusted with the thought that they might be on camera, but now that they were here he had little choice. He just was not sure whether or not he could perform – while being watched by – "unknown persons". He definitely was going to make sure that she was totally exposed before he was. He pulled the sweatshirt and bra up over her head and then went for the pants. She gave him no resistance. She continued with long loving kisses.

As he pushed her pants down she snickered. "You can't get the pants over the snow boots." She sat up and turned so that she was sitting between his legs with her feet on his chest. As he started undoing her shoelaces she reached down and started undoing his laces. She laid back and pulled his boots and socks off. He was doing the same to her boots. After he got her boots off he pulled her pants off and threw them against the wall. She got up on her knees and started unbuckling his pants while giggling.

After putting on their XXX-rated performance, they rested quietly. She way laying on top of him. After several minutes, she pushed herself up on her elbows. "Hey, do you want to go for a walk?"

He looked up at her like she had lost her mind. "Now?"

"Why not?" She gave him a quick kiss. "We can possibly find some place to get something to eat and then come back."

He stretched. "Let's do a quick clean up and then we'll go."

After taking a quick lukewarm shower (together) they got

dressed.

Before they left the room, he decided to see for himself if they were under some kind of observation. He remembered seeing a scene in some spy movie where the agent had left a small clue that only he knew about, so that he could find out if he was being watched. He acted like he was scratching his arm and pulled a hair out. He kept careful track of the hair by keeping it under his fingernail. When he zipped his suitcase back up, he placed the hair in the zipper in the corner part of the zipper. He then sat down next to his suitcase and watched her getting dressed. He acted like he was just running his finger around the perimeter of the suitcase, but actually scratched a few marks in the table that the suitcase was sitting on, and memorized where the suitcase was in conjunction with the scratches.

She had taken her time drying off as if she were trying to give him (or somebody else) an additional peep show. She finally started getting dressed. He watched her pull up her panties. It was an off white color. She put on a matching bra and asked him to fasten the clasp. He walked over and as he was fastening it he noticed that the strap had a four hook and eyelet setup. One of the hooks was missing. He guessed that three out of four would still hold the thing on without too much of a problem. She put on a pair of semi-tattered blue jeans, a sweatshirt and sneakers.

They put their coats on and exited the room. They walked around for about twenty minutes.

Bradley growled and shook his head. "Light gray, dark gray, dull gray, blue-gray, drab gray, puke gray...gray-gray. They can't even come up with black or white."

They continued walking while he complained about the colors. It seemed to him that she was doing everything to steer him in a definite direction. They ended up near some subway station. He was ready to walk on by, however, she would not allow it. She kept on pulling him into the station.

"Come on, let's go in here," she urged.

He huffed. "What's so special about public transportation?"

She turned to him momentarily with a miffed look on her face. The expression changed and she gave him a strained smile. "They'll probably have a public restroom in here and I need to go… now."

'Typical,' he thought. 'We came out here to find a restaurant and she needs a crapper instead.' He shrugged and went in without a spoken comment.

She took a very direct path straight to the public restroom. He had the definite impression that she had been here before and knew her way around. He decided not to say anything about it because they might be taped as well as filmed.

He stood by the door and nonchalantly looked around. Standing on the other side of the main plaza of the station was the blonde man with the scraggly handlebar moustache. Bradley would not have recognized the man if it had not been for that extremely sorry looking moustache. 'Yes, boys and girls, we are definitely under scrutiny,' he thought. Now, he did feel a little nervous. He wondered if Mr. Moustache was the intended person to whom they were putting on their performance.

She took a long time doing her business. When she finally came out she had a bright look on her face. She kissed him and said: "Let's go find a restaurant."

Again, she seemed to know exactly where she was going. They found a restaurant where (Surprise!) the waiter spoke very good English. He gave a few instructions on the menu and information on what was what. Bradley found out that these people consume a large amount of turnips, potatoes and vodka.

The restaurant itself was somewhat amazing in regards to other things that had been seen elsewhere in this city. There were colors in here that were something other than gray. There were small plates that were white and had some red floral design on them. There were napkins that were yellow. The tablecloths were a darker shade of yellow. There was a bar on one side of the establishment that was brown and had several different colors of bottles of liquor behind the bar.

They ordered and while they were waiting for the food, again, Bradley saw the blonde man with the scraggly handlebar moustache sitting at a table in the restaurant. The man was drinking coffee and did everything he could to not make eye contact with Bradley. Bradley did everything he could to maintain full eye contact with "Comrade Moustache".

After they finished eating, he was still not sure just exactly what he had eaten. He thought he ordered some kind of veal. Was it even meat? He also was no sure what kind of vegetables were on the plate as well. He was belching up a very strange taste in his mouth all the way back to the hotel.

They arrived back in their room. He took a quick glance at his suitcase. The hair was gone and the suitcase was not sitting exactly where it had been when they left. He shook his head. The hidden hair thing actually worked.

She started her frisky routine. His stomach had settled down, for the most part, so he went along with it. She had already kicked her shoes off so he did not have to worry about those gyrations. He slowly pulled her sweatshirt off and then the pants. He got behind her and got ready to start unhooking her bra. He stopped for a moment and then did everything he could to hide his surprise. This was not the same bra that he had hooked up before their little walk. This one had four eyelets and intact hooks. The other one had silver hooks – this one had gold. The back area showed very little signs of wear. The first one had shown a little fraying on the side with the eyelets. What had she done in that bathroom? That was the only time she was out of his sight and could have possibly done something with…changing her underwear.

She cleared her throat. "What's taking so long, honey?"

He swallowed. "I'm…uh…doing it slowly…uh…you know, anticipation." He chuckled nervously. "Slowly, so that we can both get warmed up with the anticipation."

She giggled playfully. "Oh. Is that it?"

He noticed that this bra – like the first one – was the same shade as her panties. Now he started getting a little more nervous. He pondered the situation. 'We're supposed to be a diversion. Does a diversion covertly change their underwear in a public restroom?'

He pushed the straps off of her shoulders and decided to go

for the gusto. He put his arms around her, cupped her breasts and squeezed.

She slapped at his hands. "Not so rough!" she said playfully. "Those things are definitely attached. They're a part of me."

Now was the time to put on a good show for the perverts. He kissed the back of her neck and then slowly slid his hands down her sides as he bent his knees. He pushed her panties down as he continued down.

After they had finished their little afternoon peep show, she suggested that they go get something to eat...again.

He looked at her confused. "Is that all we're going to do here is eat and screw?"

She cooed at him. "Come one Sweetie, you said that I was too cold. I'm trying to be affectionate and...well, be what you want me to be in bed."

He was very tired, however, he knew that he had to keep up with the charade. "We need to talk as well. There's more to marriage than humping in the sack. You know that a strong relationship is based on communication...not copulation."

She gave him a long loving kiss. When she pulled up for air, she smiled. "One thing at a time, honey," she said in an alluring voice. "Remember that we're still trying to have a baby." She gave him another kiss. "Let's go get something to eat while you're replenishing your little soldiers...and your strength."

They continued the charade for two more days. Taking walks, eating and copulation. The conversations that they had were a few variations on ramblings that they had rehearsed back in Frankfurt. He had been going along with all of the sex because he figured that he might not have another opportunity – sexually – like this again. Why not make the most of it while he could? Why not? Because the sex was getting routine and mundane because he was getting so much of it.

On the positive side he did notice that his belt was getting a little loose. The food tasted a little strange so he was eating less. The Russian beer tasted horrid and he could not stand vodka, so he was drinking a lot less. He was doing a lot of "abdominal crunches" when they were copulating. Maybe the "sexercise" does really work.

After a morning delight they were headed out to get something to eat. As they rounded a corner, someone came running up behind them and Bradley felt a sharp pain in the back of his head. He pitched forward and was so stunned that he did not have a chance to try breaking his fall. He felt his face hit the sidewalk. He tried to push himself up, both arms were grabbed by…someone and he was pulled up in a very rough manner. The man with the scraggly handlebar moustache was standing in front of him saying something but his ears were ringing too loud to hear anything he could understand. The world started spinning and he could not focus on anything. He thought he heard Marie hollering. He thought he heard a man speaking angrily. He thought he saw a few more different shades of gray, then tunnel vision, then he passed out.

6

Back in Frankfurt, Germany, Bates was sitting at his desk reading a report. It was more of the same stuff that he had seen before and was the entire reason that he had sent the agents to Russia. There was nothing new here and it disgusted him.

He picked up another report that made him worry. A certain ally had sent forty-two agents behind the iron curtain to check on the same information. Thirty-eight of the agents had been captured or killed in the first forty-eight hours after their arrival. The status of the other four was unknown...to anyone on this side of the border. He put the report down and grunted in disgust.

He looked at pictures on the wall. Pictures of some of the people that had been caught or killed in the line of duty. There were three of them who might spend the rest of their lives in a Siberian gulag. Nineteen of them were dead. Two were missing and...no sign of them for several years. He hated it when he added a new picture up there. He kept them as a reminder of just how dangerous this job was.

He shook his head. "Where did we get this information...on those...thirty-eight captured agents?"

His Aide, Charles Burke, looked up. "We've been listening to a radio signal...that the Russians think..." He snickered. "...is secure. We broke the code on it within thirty minutes of them first using it in their secret broadcasting. We've been doing everything we can to make sure that no one, absolutely no one, but us, knows that the code has been broken…by us."

Bates sighed. "Have any of the other countries…had any similar tragedies with their personnel that they sent out?"

Burke hung his head and scratched his left ear. He looked up out from under his eyebrows. "All of them have had many… tragedies." He raised his head up. "Both the gulags and the cemeteries are filling up fast."

Bates closed his eyes. "Are there any reports…that talk about any of the three…that I sent in?"

"No, Sir, there are no reports on any of ours…yet."

"Are you sure?"

Burke snarled back. "According to what we've found out, the Russians have certain agents identified with numbers. We use code names, but, they use numbers."

"How does that help?"

"We sent in an agent with the code name of 'Haggis'. They call him 27469. We haven't heard anything about 27469. We sent in an agent with the code name 'Trombone'. They call him 30012. We haven't heard anything about 30012. We sent in an agent with the code name of 'Wintergreen'. Wintergreen went in…plus one. They call her 44021. We haven't heard anything on her…or the plus one, which they *would* assign a number to…if they find and/or capture him."

Bates picked up the other report and got ready to read it. "That doesn't give me any reason to relax. They might…just change their coding system...and leave us in the dark...just to be facetious."

Burke laughed. "You've heard about that new linguistics genius that we have. We put fifteen different codes in front of him. It took him less than half a day to break all of them. Whitworth, over in Office 7, came up with another one, that was so complicated that it took him four days to print out a message with that code. The genius broke it in five hours."

Bates frowned and nodded. "I hadn't heard of him...until now. Does this genius have a name?"

Burke picked up his coffee. "His code name is...Yakitty-Yak." He took a sip and put the cup back down.

"Not very original. Someone could figure that one out. A code name is supposed to be misleading."

Bates picket up another report. He grunted in disgust as he read it. Each paragraph brought new concern about the safety of his agents. The number of agents that had been snagged and had either been killed in a gun battle, fist fight or committed suicide was incredible. The numbers were staggering. "Almost two hundred western agents...are dead?"

Burke nodded. "That's what is says," he admitted sadly.

"How could they have known...unless they have...a mole... somewhere inside...?"

"That is one horrible possibility," said Burke. "The problem there...they would have to have a mole in all of the agencies... everywhere and...they're all ratting our people out...rather well."

A courier walked into the office with an envelope. "I have a message here...Samuel Bates...For Your Eyes Only."

Bates raised his right hand. "Here."

The courier walked to his desk. "May I see some identification please?"

Bates pulled out his ID card and his passport. He handed them to the courier."

After the scrutiny was over, the courier had Bates sign for the envelope and he departed.

Bates opened the envelope and read the message. He leaned back in his chair growling.

"Uh-oh," said Burke. "That doesn't sound too good."

"Agent Haggis...is dead. The message...was intercepted... by our Yakitty-Yak. 27469 got in a shoot-out with the Russians. He blew his brains out...with his last bullet." Bates slammed the enveloped down on the desk. "His contacts confirmed the report... less than an hour ago." He closed his eyes and clenched his teeth. "We've got a man down...permanently."

Two hours later another courier walked in. Bates groaned in disgust as he was handed another envelope. He read the new information and shook his head. "Well...at least this is a better kind of news."

Burke frowned. "Good news...like what? I'm not on that committee, Sir."

"Agent Trombone...otherwise known as 30012...got away from the Soviet bully-boys that were following him. He grabbed a boat...and has escaped across the Black Sea to Turkey. He's already reported in...at some Turkish safe house...he's safe."

"NO!" I don't like the trend. If there's a way... get hold of Wintergreen...we need to get her out of there as well...especially since she has that plus one, with as great haste as we can muster."

"What's so special about the plus one?"

Bates gave Burke a disgusted look. "By using him, we violated the law! There was an Act of Congress that was put into law...a long time ago...in the 1880's. *Posse Comitatus*! We're not allowed to just grab some member of the US Military...for any civilian...action...unless we first obtain permission from the Secretary of Defense."

Burke looked back wide-eyed. "We...didn't?" He looked very worried.

"No, we didn't. If Wintergreen...or plus one...get captured or killed...I have to call the Whitehouse and..." He threw his hands up in disgust. "I have to say...Mister President...we broke the law. Sorry to inform you this way...Lyndon...but...I know you don't like silly messes...and especially since you'll have to turn this one over to that new guy...Richard...when he gets inaugurated...in a couple of months...but we've got a member of the United States Air Force, that we *snatched* from an Air Base in Germany, and sent him on a covert operation...on the other side of the iron curtain... without *any* authorization...from you or anyone else in Washington DC. Oh, yes, he was in the company of one of our agents...but...

we never bothered to get any authorization to use him…as a…toy puppet. Now…the Russians are going to have a field day with their propaganda. You're going to leave the Whitehouse with egg…and Russian feces…all over your face. Sorry about that. Oh, by the way, have a nice day."

Burke looked rather worried. "Is there any way to get hold of…Wintergreen…and get her and plus one…out of there…safely?"

Bates sat there grumbling. "How should I know? The only thing that we know…for sure is…she's somewhere in or near Moscow…I think."

"Aren't there any…of her contacts…that we could contact to let her know?"

"We'd have to wait until we hear from them and… communicate it to them at that time. Other than that…we've got no way of contacting her," Bates said in a lackadaisical manner.

"Let's hope that we hear something…good…soon," Burke said encouragingly.

Bates sighed and shook his head.

Less than an hour later the courier brought another envelope.

Bates stared at it for almost twenty minutes before he opened it. He read it carefully, hoping that some silly miracle would happen and the words on the page would change…somehow. Then he just hung his head.

Burke was itching to ask, however, he was afraid to. He knew that he would find out eventually so he just sat there waiting… on pins and needles.

Bates looked up. "44021...and a newly designated...98174... have just been taken into custody. 44021 is Wintergreen...and 98174...is..." He looked up at the ceiling. "...I give him the code name...Patsy!" He laid his head down on the desk. "And it might just be the end of my career."

Burke swallowed. "What should I do?"

Bates looked up. "We might both...get ready to clean out... our desks."

Burke pursed his lips. "Just how bad could it get?"

Bates sighed. "Being a member of the US Military... they could take their propaganda machines and...turn it into an invasion. He wasn't in uniform...but he didn't have permission to be there. They could still try to say that it *is* an invasion...by the US Military...into the peaceful, fun-loving Democratic country of the Soviet Union."

Before getting ready to leave for the day, another courier came in with an envelope.

Burke looked around confused. "Now what? The only assets that we had there...are used up. We've got nothing left...and we haven't sent anyone else."

Bates shook he head as he looked at the envelope. "I don't know what to think...until I open this thing." He tore it open and read the note. He dropped it on the table and let out a disgusted noise. "The whole lousy thing was a red herring! The Soviets leaked a bunch of crap about...something that doesn't exist...never existed.

They let out something…that they knew would get our attention and everybody else…and we bit…along with all of our allies…we bit. Every agent that went in…those Russians were waiting for anyone who was entering their country…and had all of them marked. We got suckered…big time!"

1

Bradley woke up sitting in a hard wooden armchair with his wrists strapped tightly to the armrests. He flexed his fingers trying to get full feeling back in his hands. He blinked his eyes several times trying to clear the cobwebs and get his vision back into focus.

Someone was talking to him, however, he could not understand what was being said. He looked up. He saw a tall man with incredibly big, bushy dark eyebrows. Standing next to Mister Eyebrows was the scraggly handlebar moustache. Bradley just sat there waiting for the other shoe to fall. He had no idea what to say if he had wanted to say anything. He shook his head several times. It did not help. It just seemed to make him a little dizzier for a few moments. He finally realized that the man was talking to him in Russian. He was probably doing that to see if Bradley could understand Russian.

"*Nicht verstehen*," said Bradley and then realized that he had just spoken German.

Eyebrows stopped speaking and looked at Moustache. Eyebrows switched to English. "Is it Russian or German that you do not understand?"

"Both," said Bradley.

Eyebrows nodded with a smirk on his face. "Then why did you say it in German?"

"Because I don't know how to say it in Russian," said

Bradley facetiously.

"Well you do understand English…so I suppose I will have to continue in that language, since you are obviously not going to let me know how much Russian you really do understand."

Bradley was still trying to clear his head. "*Da* and *nyet*," he said flatly.

The two Russians conversed with each other for a few moments and then left the room.

A minute later, Marie was bodily thrown into the room. She landed in a heap and then stood up facing the door. "I ain't no spy!" she screamed. She went to the door and tried to open it. Locked. She pounded on the door a few times. "Hey, you stupid Russkies, I ain't no spy! What kinda crap are you tryin' to pull?" She stood there fuming for a few moments and then turned around. She finally saw Bradley and looked at him in shock. "Hey, Baby, what happened to you?"

He looked at her in total disbelief. "Huh?"

"Your face is all tore up," she said looking very concerned.

He frowned and felt a little pain on the right side of his face as the muscles moved. "What the…?"

She came closer to him and looked closely at the right side of his face. "It looks like someone took sandpaper to your face. What'd they do?"

"I think that happened when I got clobbered on the street. I broke my fall with my face."

She looked shocked. "Oh, well you shoulda used your hands."

He wanted to slap her. If he had not been bound to the chair he could have had the chance. He simply scowled. "I didn't have the chance. Somebody cold-cocked me and I was half out on the way down."

"Well, Baby, they're sayin' that we're spies," she said innocently. "Why would they say that? Is there somethin' that you're not tellin' me?"

He looked at her incredulously. "If I was a spy, do you think that someone could have snuck up on me like that? If I was a spy, don't you think that I would have some kind of crazy little spy gizmos with me? If I was a spy, don't you think that I would have had some unexplained private time away from you? Huh?"

She looked terrified. "I dunno," she said in a blank manner.

"Great idea you had...let's go somewhere that we don't know nuthin' about and all we'll have to cling to is each other. Yeah! Great! Now what do we do?"

"Well they can't do nuthin' to us cause we didn't do nuthin'."

"I know that you and know that – do they know that?"

At that moment, Eyebrows and four other men came into the room. Two of the men were dressed in military uniforms. One of them was looking over Bradley and Marie's passports.

Eyebrows had a big smile on his face. "Your contacts, here in the Soviet Union have confessed. You might as well make it easier on yourself and confess as well."

"I don't wear contact lenses," said Marie. "What are you talking about?"

Bradley looked around the room. "Who are you talking to? The only people that I have had any contact with is waiters and bellhops." He looked at Marie. "Have you contacted anybody?"

She shook her head. "The only people we talked to, other than each other, is them customs people that tore our luggage apart, the taxi driver, the man at the desk at the hotel and, like he said, waiters and bellhops. Who is these contacts and who did they confess to?"

"Stop playing silly games with me!" Eyebrows switched his gaze back and forth between the two of them. "I know that you are CIA spies. I know this. You cannot deny this truth."

"Wanna bet?" said Marie indignantly. "We ain't got no secret stuff on us, we ain't been talkin' to nobody and only stuff we got to take out of this country is the stuff we came in with."

Eyebrows grunted. "The...*stuff*...you came into the Soviet Union with will have rotted away by the time you two get out of jail."

The five Russians conversed back and forth for a few minutes. Marie walked over to hug Bradley. One of the Russian uniforms quickly ran up to Marie and threw her away from Bradley. He looked down at Marie. "You! No talking to him. You no touch him."

She cowered on the floor.

Bradley decided to play his role as "loving husband". "You

better watch that crap! I'm gonna report this...all of this to the US Embassy at the earliest possible opportunity."

Eyebrows laughed. "Spies do not have any right to talk to any Embassy anywhere in the world. Embassies are to remain neutral and don't talk to or listen to spies and saboteurs. If they want to continue as an Embassy...they will have nothing to do with you."

Bradley felt his dander rising a little. It almost seemed easy to get into character. "What am I supposed to be spying on? Huh? Russian restaurants? That fleabag dump of a hotel? That jalopy taxi? What?"

Eyebrows bent over with his face near Bradley's. "As I said: Your contacts have already confessed. We already know why you are here. Your mission has failed. Confess! It will go easier on you at your trial. It might mean a little less time in a Soviet gulag."

Bradley sighed. "I can't confess to something that I know nothing about." He shook his head. "And I don't know anything about any contacts. The only person that I've seen more than once...is that idiot with the sorry looking excuse for a moustache. If someone, here in Russia, confessed to something about me...or her...you tortured them into confessing to a lie...which is what you commie pigs do best."

"I didn't do nuthin' either," whined Marie with a shaky voice.

One of the other men walked up closer to Bradley. He was medium height, rather obese and his cheap black suit did not fit very well. His breath reeked of vodka. His jowls shook a little as he talked in a rather high pitched voice. "You can confess to nothing eh? You did not do nothing, eh? You have no secret information on you, eh? You have no funny little spy toys, eh? We find out now." He looked at Marie. "Search her – completely!"

The other four men slowly walked up to her with menacing grins on their faces.

Eyebrows held out his hand. "Your shirt – remove it."

She looked back at them wide-eyed in shock. "What? Here? Now? Aren't you gonna get some women in here…to search me?"

"You are in the Soviet Union. We treat everybody equal here. We do not have decadent laws that allow all criminals to get away with their crimes. When we prosecute someone, we use laws that put criminals, like you, in jail. Man can search woman, woman can search man. We believe in total equality…unlike the decadent imperialists of the west. We are here now and we did not see any reason to bring a woman." He moved his hand closer to her. "Give me your shirt, NOW!"

Bradley knew that he had to play the decent husband. He was momentarily distracted when he thought for a moment: 'Hey, where are our coats?' He dismissed the thought as quickly as he could. They had obviously taken the coats and torn them apart by now. He growled at Eyebrows. "Don't you have any decency? What kind of stupid game are you trying to pull here?" He tried to do a little standing and/or rocking the thing to pull his act off and discovered that the chair he was in, was bolted to the floor. 'So much for that idea,' he thought.

"I'm not takin' my clothes off in front of a bunch of strange men," complained Marie. "It just ain't right."

Eyebrows slapped her. The slap spun her around and she hit the wall before she fell to the floor.

'Why don't you do one of your kicks or punches now?' thought Bradley. 'That should really convince them that we're *not* spies.'

She started crying. None of them showed any pity on their faces.

"Stop this nonsense! Give me your shirt!" hollered Eyebrows.

"Oh you just wait," said Bradley. "The Embassy is gonna get an ear-load of this."

One of the uniforms smacked Bradley in the back of the head. "Don't worry, spy! You will get your turn...and we still have proof enough so that you don't get to talk to Embassy."

"You're gonna get your turn being embarrassed when I get through with all of this nonsense that you're spouting, commie!"

Marie sniffled as she slowly pulled her sweatshirt off and handed it to Eyebrows. She quickly covered herself up with her arms.

'Nice touch,' thought Bradley. He wondered how she was able to blush on cue. Her face looked like she was really embarrassed. She was *real* good at this stuff.

Eyebrows gave the shirt to one of the uniforms. That man pulled a magnifying glass out of a pocket and started looking over the hems. Eyebrows turned back to Marie. He held out his hand again. "Your pants!"

She pulled her sneakers off and started undoing her blue jeans. The fat one came over and kicked her shoes off to the side. The other uniform picked up a shoe and started shredding it with a knife. Marie pushed her pants down and squatted as she did. She looked up with terror in her eyes at Eyebrows. After she had pulled the pants off kicked them towards Eyebrows. She pulled her knees up to her chest and it looked to Bradley as if her face got even redder.

The fifth man in the room was much older. He had white hair and looked a little frail. He stood there with his hands behind his back, watching everything that was going on. He walked up to Bradley. "You have nothing to say?"

Bradley was doing everything he could to stay angry. "I'm taking note. I'm watching everything that's going on so I can report this outrage to my Embassy. Any more stupid questions, YUH STUPID IMPERIALISTIC COMMIE PIG!"

The old man turned away and walked back towards the door. He turned back to what was going on in the room and continued watching.

Marie's other shoe was destroyed as well. The man doing the cutting then went over to the one with the sweatshirt and said something in Russian. The one with the shirt pointed at the pants. The knife disappeared into a pocket, the uniform went over, picked up the pants, pulled out a magnifying glass and started looking closely at the hems.

The close search of the shirt took quite a while. When he was finished with it he simply dropped it on the floor and looked at Eyebrows.

Eyebrows went over to Marie. He held out his hand again. "Next article of clothing."

"Oh no," she whined. She shook her head and tears started running down her cheeks.

"If you want, I can get someone to help you," said Eyebrows.

She looked down at herself. She looked up at him angrily, reached down and pulled her socks off. She threw them at his face. He caught one of them and the other one hit him in the chin. He gave her a disgusted look, reached down, picked up the fallen sock and took them to the first uniform. The socks did not take long to search.

Eyebrows walked back over to Marie and held out his hand again. She looked around helplessly and started crying again. She got up on her knees and faced the wall. She reached back and unfastened her bra. She shrugged out of the bra and while still facing the wall, she threw the bra over her shoulder and sat down sobbing.

Bradley was still doing everything he could to look angry and indignant. He could see out of the corner of his eyes that the old man was studying every move that Bradley and Marie were making. Bradley decided that right now, the easiest thing he could do was just bow his head and do a little snarling.

Bradley heard something being torn. He looked up quickly. The bra was being shredded just like the shoes. After the uniform finished destroying the bra he threw the pieces on the floor and looked at Eyebrows.

Marie had only one piece of clothing left. She looked up at Eyebrows whimpering pitifully. He held out his hand. She bowed her head and started sobbing again. She got up on her knees, faced the wall again and pushed her panties down. She fell to her right and used her legs to push the panties off as she moved herself up against the wall, facing it.

Bradley started looking around the room at all the Russians. His teeth and fists were clenched tight. "Oh are you gonna pay for this," he said through controlled angry breaths. "Not only are you commies…you're perverts as well. And then you have the gall to say that Americans are decadent? I'm lookin' at a bunch of commie PERVERTS!"

The old man was standing by the door. He reached back without turning and knocked on the door. A moment later a woman came in putting on surgical gloves. The woman strode purposely towards Marie. This woman was wearing a very drab gray outfit (big surprise, gray), some kind of clod-hopping shoes and her brown hair was tied back in a bun on the back of her head. Bradley did not have to guess what was going to happen next.

Eyebrows grabbed Marie's arm and pulled her away from the wall. She started screaming. The uniforms each grabbed a leg and pulled them apart. The Russian woman knelt down between Marie's legs.

Bradley just turned his head away with his eyes closed as tight as his fists. He was getting a little tired from acting angry. He did not know how much longer he could keep it up. He knew that it was all he had left as far as proving any form of innocence.

Marie was screaming at the top of her lungs now. She was pleading for them to stop and calling them all kinds of nasty names.

When the screaming stopped, Bradley opened his eyes and turned to look back at Marie. She was kneeling, facing into a corner and whimpering.

The Russian woman pulled the gloves off. She looked at Eyebrows, shrugged, shook her head and left the room.

The two uniforms had finished looking (and destroying) her clothing. They kicked all the pieces of clothing – intact and shredded – back at Marie. She flinched and yelped when her pants hit her. She looked back and saw her clothing laying behind her. She reached back and grabbed the pants. She stood up as she pulled the pants on. She squatted back down, reached back, grabbed the sweatshirt and pulled it back on. She fastened the pants and then sifted through the shredded remains of the other stuff, found her panties and shoved them in her pocket. She then put her socks on and looked fearfully at Eyebrows. She sat back down in the corner, pulled her knees up to her chest and sat there whimpering and sniffing.

Eyebrows walked behind Bradley. Bradley figured that it was now his turn to suffer complete humiliation. He expected a hard blow to the back of his head at any moment. Instead, Eyebrows came back to Bradley's front, carrying a chair. Eyebrows placed the chair in front of Bradley and sat down. He folded his arms and let out a long sigh. "Who are you?"

Bradley was totally surprised at this different treatment. "Huh?"

Eyebrows leaned closer. "Who are you?"

Bradley glanced around at some of the other men in the room. Through his puzzlement he finally mustered the courage to talk. He tried to talk and all that came out was a gargle. He cleared his throat and said: "Bradley F. Dooley. Just like it says on my passport."

Eyebrows sighed again. "I can be a patient man. Sometimes though, I am not so patient. We know who she is. She has been in the Soviet Union before. We found your fingerprints in the hotel room and compared them with all known spies. Hers we found easily. Yours…" Eyebrows shrugged. "…we did not. Who are you?"

Bradley felt a cold chill go down his back. He tried to remain poker-faced. "Bradley Franklin Dooley, and I don't know what you're talking about with this fingerprint thing. I'm no spy. If she's one…that's news to me."

Eyebrows narrowed his eyes. "This is not her first spy mission in the Soviet Union. We can prove that she has been here at least two times before. We cannot find your fingerprints. So this is your first spy mission. Who are you and why did you come here? What is your mission of sabotage here in the Soviet Union?"

Bradley turned back to look at Marie. She was still keeping up the act of a terrified tourist. She had stopped sniffling but that was all of the act that had stopped. He turned back to Eyebrows. "Bradley Franklin Dooley…and I don't know what else I could possibly tell you."

The fat one walked up and stood next to Eyebrows. "We have a special place for spies. If you don't want to give us the information easily – we get it the hard way...but we still get it. We will take you to our special place now. Then you will spend the next twenty or thirty...or forty years in a gulag in Siberia. If you cooperate, it might not be so long." He smiled.

8

Bradley was released from the chair. Now that those tight bonds were not on his wrists he was able to get full feeling back in his hands. He wondered if that was the last satisfying feeling that he would have...for a long time.

The two prisoners were trussed up in chains. A belly band was put on each one of them. Handcuffs were hooked through the belly band and then around the wrists. Another set was on the ankles. Bradley went through the ordeal with his jaws tight. He did not look at Marie nor did he hear her whimpering, crying or complaining any more.

Marie was taken out first, between two uniforms, followed immediately by two uniforms with Bradley in tow. They were led down a long hallway, turned to some double doors, through the doors to the outside.

As soon as they went outside, Marie let out a slight cry of surprise. Bradley found out why she had yelped when he went through the doors. The wind was blowing hard, making it bitterly cold. All of the Russians were wearing thick, heavy coats, big sable hats, thick gloves and heavy boots, so they were not affected very much by that cold. The two prisoners were being led to a large van and in the short time it took to get to the van, both were shivering badly. Once inside the van, the temperature was not much warmer, but there was no wind. They were seated, side by side, on a very cold metal side facing bench seat and strapped in.

Eyebrows climbed into the van. He placed a pad on the bench seat on the opposite side of the van and sat down. He held up a large ring of keys, jingled them and smiled. "I bet you want to get your hands on these. No matter. Even if you do, you are not going to go anywhere Mister Dooley…if that really is your name. I doubt that it is. We will find out in good time." He dropped the keys in a large pocket on the right side of his coat.

Another Russian climbed in and sat down next to Eyebrows. This man had not been in the room during Marie's humiliation, so Bradley had no idea who this new flaxen haired man was. This man just sat down and stared at nothing in particular.

Four more Russians in uniform climbed into the back of the van, three men and a woman. Each one of them had a rifle with bayonets ready for business. They all stared at Marie and Bradley with anger in their eyes. Bradley and Marie both looked back with complete disgust and contempt in their eyes.

Bradley could see that there was a vehicle in front and one in back. They were lining up a nice little convoy for the ride to… oblivion. 'Let me have my mundane life back,' he thought. 'Why did she have to pick me? Dooley! Yes, that was my name. Now you can call me Diversionary Schmuck!' He bowed his head. His heart felt like it had fallen into his stomach. He was beginning to really dread what lay ahead.

Marie sighed. All of the planning to use her "fool" as a diversion and it blew up in her face. She had a good idea as to where they were headed. After the drugs and/or torture that they were going to endure, she figured that the fool would spill his guts and they would probably give him just a short stretch at a gulag. She figured that – if she lived that long – she would not get out of the gulag until the next century.

The back door to the van was closed. The four guards sat down – two on each side. The van was started and then move slowly forward. Bradley noticed that the air inside the van was getting warmer already. So much for freezing to death, before arriving at a gulag. No, these commies wanted their prizes to stay alive for a while longer. At least until they could turn their minds into jelly from torturing and doping them.

Bradley was too angry to look at Marie. He stared out the front of the van as they moved along some city streets. They moved past several high-rise tenement buildings that were all some shade of gray. All too soon they were out in the country. Finally he was seeing something other than gray. Mostly brown and white, from leafless trees and snow. He still wondered if these people knew that there were colors other than gray. Pasture land soon changed to hills and then, after a while, larger hills or possibly mountains. The scenery might have been pleasant to look at if it were not for the horror that he was headed for.

There was nothing that he could tell them. Maybe he should just fold and tell them everything that had happened. He was an unwilling sucker on this unfortunate escapade. How long would it be before they believed him? Right now, he did not really care what was going to happen to Marie...*if* that was her real name.

They were rolling along the melancholy trip when the driver looked up to his right and hollered something. All of the guards and Eyebrows looked startled and then looked up to the front of the van. Bradley could not tell what was getting them so excited until he saw a boulder go rolling across the road and shoved the lead vehicle over the left side of the road.

A tremendously loud bang was heard inside the van and it suddenly lurched sideways violently to the left. Then it was utter mayhem as the van was now tumbling down the side of a mountain. Bradley closed his eyes as he was being bombarded by bodies and other debris inside the van as it tumbled. He heard grunts and screams of pain as they were jolted and bounced around. He had no idea how many times they had flipped when the van finally came to a sliding stop, laying on its side.

Bradley could hear nothing now except someone's labored breathing. He opened his eyes and felt very dizzy. Someone was laying across Bradley's stomach. Someone who was not moving at all. Bradley realized that the body on top of him was Eyebrows. The uniformed personnel were all wearing brown coats, while the man on top of him had on that black coat. He also realized that the van had come to rest where he was laying on his back.

When his head finally quit spinning he kept listening...for anything. The labored breathing was to his left and was coming from someone hidden behind another non-moving body.

The way that he was cuffed, his hands were only inches apart. The problem for him was that the chain on the cuffs was wound around the belly band, giving him very little motion. He used what he could to manipulate the motionless body on top of him. He had to get to that pocket where all of the keys were located. It took several exhausting minutes before he finally obtained the keys. Now he had to go through the arduous task of one-key-at-a-time, until he finally found the key that released the cuff on his left wrist. He lay there panting for a few moments. After unlocking the cuff on his right wrist, he pushed the lifeless body of Eyebrows off and unhooked the "seatbelt". Now he had to get into a very awkward position in order to free his ankles.

By the time he had all of his shackles off he suddenly realized that the labored breathing had stopped. He listened intensely and heard nothing. That was when he noticed that the van had been badly misshapen in the tumble and the back doors were not in place anymore. One door was missing entirely. The other was bent out of shape. He could get out...if he wanted to...and do...what?

He stood up to survey the carnage. Marie was still strapped in where she had been and was unconscious. There was a large bruise on her forehead that appeared to be the shape of a rifle butt. Eyebrows and three of the guards were not moving. Three? Where were the others? The only thing he could imagine was that somehow, someone had been thrown out through the damaged doors.

He looked forward to the driver. That man was hanging half-way out of the shattered windshield – and not moving.

He checked to see if he could figure out who had been breathing so hard and was suddenly silent. The only thing that he could figure was that it had to be the female guard who, somehow during the tumble, got a bayonet rammed deep into her chest. The woman's dead eyes were staring blindly, straight up. Her mouth was wide open...and filled with blood. The woman had either died from a knife wound through the heart or she had drowned in her own blood. Bradley had no time to feel sorry for the woman.

He stumbled a little as he crawled out of the van. He started to shiver a little so he went back inside and got one of the coats from a guard. He found a pair of spectacles in the pocket of the coat and decided to use them to find out if anyone was still alive.

He placed a lens under Marie's nose. The lens instantly fogged up. Okay, she is still breathing. No one else in the van was breathing. He put the glasses back in the pocket. No telling – he might need them later. For what he had no idea, however, he kept them anyway.

He picked up one of the big fur hats, put it on and headed out of the van again. He quickly discovered that all three vehicles were in the bottom of a very deep gully. He looked up and could not tell where the road was. He could not tell how far they had tumbled.

The place looked like the aftermath of a battle. All three vehicles were badly mangled. There were several bodies strewn about. A few of them were in very unnatural positions. He did the lens test on all of them and then chuckled. The propaganda about seatbelts was correct. He and Marie had been the only ones strapped in and now they were the only ones who were still alive. The only reason she was hurt was because she had been hit in the head by some unrestrained flying debris.

He looked back up at the cliff that they had just come tumbling down from. He could see several places where the snow was now missing on some large boulders. He could not tell how far they had fallen, however, it was no small distance. He had nothing to set the scale because all he saw were a few boulders jutting out of the snow and that did not really help. All he was sure of was the fact that it was far enough for the vehicles and personnel to get totally mangled.

'What do I do now?' he thought. 'Do I wait for another convoy to come along or...?' He looked back at the van. There was a woman in there who had not died from the crash. She died from a knife wound. Would there be a murder charge? Why not? There was no way that the Russians would believe that it was a result of the accident. If they had not been escorting two *dangerous* spies, the accident would never have happened and the woman would be alive somewhere else, probably guzzling vodka. They would figure out some way of putting the blame right in the lap of Bradley Franklin Dooley. He snorted in exasperation. "Wouldn't you know it?" he growled. "It had to be a woman who condemns me. Of all the people who got killed in the accident...a woman had to be the one who looks like she was murdered...and it looks like I finished her off...because she somehow lived through the accident. Forget the fact that I was cuffed and restrained and tied down to the vehicle...all they'll say is...she was unconscious while I got out of the restraints...and then murdered her after I got free. Why does it always have to be a woman that...gives me the biggest problems... even in Russia?"

Three men in the lead truck, eight in the prison van and three in the rear truck. Fourteen dead Russians. He decided to think of other things rather than what the "consequences" might be.

He breathed a long hard sigh and started an inventory of everything that was here...other than a pile of dead bodies.

He went back into the van and noticed that Marie's lips were turning blue. Well it was cold and it was also beginning to snow. He pulled coats off of several dead bodies and used them to bundle her up after he went through the frustrating task of finding the right keys to get rid of her shackles.

In his searches of the three vehicles, he found, what appeared to be, some kind of a sled in the lead vehicle. It was (for the most part), about seven feet long and slid along very easily on snow on what seemed to be built in runners on the bottom. He also found some snow shoes, food, a bottle of vodka and tons of ammunition.

There was not very much that was useful in the prison van, except that he now had a pretty good sized arsenal and a lot of very warm clothing.

The third vehicle had a little more food, vodka, binoculars and rifles.

He also found something very strange as he was going through several dozen pockets. He found a compass. It was identical to a compass that an aunt had given him for Christmas years ago. It was part of a set that had included a toy rifle, toy pistol, plastic bayonet and…a compass. Written in English on the back of the compass was the symbol and slogan for the "Combat Commando Battle Set". He wondered just how bad off was the Russian military, when they had to use an American toy…to function properly.

He went back to check on Marie. She was finally awake. He was confused as to why she had not made any attempt at getting up. She was looking around with some fear in her eyes. Her mouth was moving, however, no sound was coming out. He pulled some of the coats off of her. He was terrified in thinking of just how badly she had been hurt in the tumble. She was able to mover her arms and legs a little, but not enough to do anything useful.

"Wonderful," he huffed. He looked up to heaven as if asking

for guidance. "Some kind of brain damage. She's still alive but she's a complete invalid. What do I do...now?"

He decided to use what little he knew of medicine and checked her out. He looked her in the eyes and saw that she was looking back into his eyes. "Follow my finger," he said. He moved it around and she followed it easily. "Okay, so you can hear me and understand. Can you talk?"

Again she moved her lips a little, however, no sound came out. Her breathing seemed normal though. What ever got damaged in her brain was not affecting her breathing...too much. She just could not talk or move on her own.

He had to try for some kind of communication. "Can you blink your eyes?"

She responded with several quick blinks. 'Yeah I can hear you, dummy,' she thought.

He nodded. "Okay, one blink for yes and two for no, got it?"

One blink. 'That's right, dummy, keep it simple. Maybe you'll remember it.'

"Are you in any pain?"

Two blinks. 'What possible difference could that make now...dummy?'

"Can you move much of anything in your body?"

She wiggled a little up and down the entire length of her body, however, she was not able to raise up in any way. She finally went totally limp and blinked twice. 'Something ain't right.'

"All right," he said in a worried manner. "I'm going to pull you on a sled."

She quickly blinked twice. 'That's insane, you dummy! Leave me here! Get out of here and…survive…as long as you can.' If she could, she would have belted him in order to knock some sense into him.

He was very shocked. "Do you want me…to leave you here?"

One blink. 'I wish I could say it! I'd leave *you* here.'

"No! I can't leave you here. Are you serious? Or are you crazy?"

One blink. 'Leave me here you bonehead,' she thought. 'I have no intention of being dragged…who knows where…until…oh, I don't want to think about it.'

He clenched his teeth and tried to think. After a few moments of contemplation he turned to her. "I am not cold-blooded enough to leave…even YOU…here to die. Also during the night it could get awfully cold. If I have someone to get close to, under a blanket, then I have a better chance of survival. Are you going to object to that?"

She stared at him for a few moments and then blinked twice. She then clenched her eyes shut. 'Now I'm a confounded bed warmer for this…woman hating jerk!'

He was wondering if she could eat. He got a chunk of some dark bread from the meager provisions. "We're going to test and see if you can eat," he told her.

She opened her eyes and looked at him angrily. One blink.

'Why not? Maybe I can eat. So how long is that going to keep me alive?' She mentally scoffed. 'Maybe you could turn me into a ventriloquist dummy. Of course...if you're the ventriloquist... which one of us is the real dummy?'

He put a piece of bread near her mouth. She could not open her mouth wide enough to engulf it. He tore off a tiny piece and put it in her mouth. She went through several odd looking movements with her mouth and then eventually swallowed.

He sighed. "Do I have to keep making them...that small?"

One blink. 'Oh terrific! Now, I'm going to have to be spoon fed...with pieces that were smaller than when I was a baby.'

After he had fed her the entire chunk, one tiny piece at a time, he decided to leave her to her own internal suffering and try to plan for who knows what – something – anything – survive.

While contemplating what to do he nearly stripped his mental gears trying to remember history lessons from school. He had heard several times about how harsh the Russian winter was. Things about Napoleon in his failed conquest or Hitler in World War II came to mind. He started thinking about what could be the best insulation from the cold. You can put on five or six coats, however, then you cannot function because you are so bundled up that movement is very restricted. He needed something a little less bulky. If only he had something like...rubber. He looked at the tires of the vehicles. He wondered if the Russians had modernized to tubeless tires. If they were going to supply their troops with American toys instead of sophisticated equipment...who knows?

He went to the overturned lead vehicle. All three vehicles

had six tires, so if they had inner tubes then he was going to have a lot of rubber from 18 tubes. He picked the easiest tire to get to and loosened the valve stem. After the whistling stopped, he broke the tire away from the rim and felt inside. Hallelujah! Inner tubes. He then went to the long task of getting all 18 tubes. Let all the air out, break the tire away and fight the tubes out. 18 inner tubes would make a lot of insulation.

Things were looking up…a little. He had a sled that he could pull her on. He had a pile of insulation that could help keep them warm. He had a pile of warm clothing that could also help keep them warm. He had a little food to start with. He had some rifles to defend himself from a possible wolf attack. He had vodka that he could use as an antiseptic. He had a compass.

If – by the grace of God – he could somehow avoid any Russian patrols and get to the border between the iron curtain countries and either West Germany, Austria, Greece or Turkey… and then who knows what might happen? He had thought of maybe even trying to head for India…oops…a mountain range…called the Himalayas.

The main drawback was that he might have to drag Marie the whole way. He hoped that she would be able to heal up enough to talk by the time they reached a border and would be able to tell him of some contact, somewhere along the border…he hoped.

He took another look around at the mess. Most of it was being covered up by a light snowfall that was coming straight down. He had wondered about leaving the bodies out in the snow…but what could he possibly do? Report it? To whom? Why? Then he started thinking: In for a penny, in for a pound. He went to each body and stripped them of all usable clothing. There was no telling what he might need, at a later date.

With all of the items that he could fit on the sled already, plus a few of the lighter items on his back, he checked the compass and started heading west. West Berlin, West Germany, Western Europe...he had no idea what he was going to do or how, however, he figured that somehow heading west would help...or at least it could not make his situation any worse than it already was.

To make sure that Marie was comfortable and insulated, he had made a lasagna out of the coats and inner tubes. Sled, then coats, then inner tubes, then more clothing, then tubes, then more clothing. A couple more layers like that and then he put Marie on top of that. He then built another lasagna on top of her. When she was alone, she only had her own body heat. At night he could share body heat and keep both of them warm. He hoped that there was enough heat to last her during the day...unless he decided to move at night.

Several of the rifles were placed in some of the layers. He had to put them somewhere and carrying all nine of them on his back was impossible.

He was amazed at how the sled would slide so easily over snow. It did not matter how heavy the sled was, it had been designed to glide over snow and it did. If he ever hit a patch of dry ground, he knew immediately. Over snow – no effort; over dirt –maximum effort...to move at all. He wanted to shake hands with the designer.

He had found some rope in one of the trucks and used it to make a harness for dragging the sled.

He had bid farewell to the crash site and was going west…to the future…whatever it held.

After the first day, he had to create a makeshift awning to put over her face. She had no way of cleaning the falling snow off of her face and could have suffocated. Once piece of the rubber and a few sticks was all it took. Every now and then he would check and move whatever snow build up was on top of the miniature awning.

Onward to the west he went with his unhappy cargo on a blind and ignorant journey. He wondered just how far he would get. How soon would the alarm been sounded? How soon would they find the crash site? If the snow kept falling for a long time, he was sure that all tracks of any type would be covered completely. But of course these people were not idiots. They would know that he would head in some kind of westerly direction. He had to avoid "all" towns and cities and people on the way…no matter what.

She lay on the sled helpless. She was really hating him even more. He would not leave her behind and he had no idea where he was going. Unless he had some uncanny way of telling what direction he was going, she knew that he would be going in circles and they could end up in Murmansk, Belgrade or Peking. The only time that a dummy like him could tell east from west was at sunup or sunset. When would he be moving and when would he be resting? They had gone through several blizzards so far. Most of them had lasted a day or two. One of them had been a total white-out, with zero visibility that lasted five days. Each blizzard had left them ravenous afterward, however, because he had huddled close to her, they had never been frozen. If she could, she would have snarled. What a way to go? 'I guess I'd have done the same thing, if I had to drag that dummy across the Russian wilderness.'

9

He was wondering just how long he would be able to avoid and evade. He was wondering how long it would take to find anything friendly. Then he scoffed. Friendly? Here in Russia? What could he possibly find in Russia…that would be friendly to his cause…against the KGB?

He was wondering how long the food would last. Food? The small amount of food that had been found at the crash site had been just a couple of sack lunches for two or three of the guards. They could not eat nothing but snow all the way to…wherever. He was going to have to do some hunting of…what? Hunt local game… without attracting attention! Real fun.

He remembered a friend that had taught him how to set up a snare for rabbits. It had worked back in Georgia, why not here in Russia. He had seen a great number of rabbits running around the area. He did not have the speed to catch them and he dared not shoot at them. Any shooting would bring all kinds of unwanted attention.

After two days and nights of going as far as he could, he found a small group of evergreens and decided to cold camp for a short span. He took what little bread he had left and used it as bait. He set the snares and went back to try to warm up by sharing body heat with Marie.

He was glad that he had brought all the extra material from the guards clothing because he found out quickly that he was going to have to clean and diaper Marie. She was totally helpless. The first time he had to do it she had a disgusted look in her eyes. After the first time, she surrendered her emotions to the inevitability of her bodily functions.

She had initially gone out of her way to make his "touch" acceptable. This was not what she had originally planned but what are you going to do about it when you are, hopefully, a *temporary* invalid? She had no way of communicating what she wanted and a yes/no marathon would not accomplish anything either. She had to just lay there and…eat whatever he could find. HE was using HER. That was not what she had originally planned. She was supposed to bring him here and if anything went wrong, run for Odessa, grab a boat and get to Turkey. Now what do you do?

After cleaning her he got close to her to share a little warmth, on and under a pile of coats and inner tubes. He heard some rustling in the brush and it made him nervous. He listened for the sound of footsteps. Nothing but more rustling. Short spurts of noise followed by silence. After a few minutes it really started bothering him. He crawled out from under the pile of coats, put a coat on, picked up a rifle and headed for the noise.

His fear turned to elation when he found that the rustling was a rabbit, caught in a snare, hanging near a tree, trying to run down the branches that it could reach. He walked over and clubbed the rabbit. He then pulled it free of the snare and wrung its neck. He picked up the bait and went to check the other snares. Another rabbit was dangling in the air from the trap but could not get near anything to hit with its paws the way the first one had. He clubbed this one as well.

Two rabbits and what do you do with them? He started thinking of saving for any possible lean times during the trek. If he killed it and kept it on top of the sled – it would freeze – then he would have to figure out a way to thaw it out. If he trussed it up so that it could not escape...it might make some unnecessary noise. That could draw attention. If he killed it and kept it warm – it could spoil. The only choice he could think of was to be gluttons while they had it and then live off of what little fat had been stored – if they came to having some lean times.

He pulled the other two snares down, picked up the precious bait and headed back to Marie.

He told her what his plans were with the food and with her blinking she gave no objection to what he was doing.

'He snared a couple of rabbits,' she thought. 'Big deal, oh great and mighty hunter. If I didn't see the rotten little rodents, I wouldn't have believed you. What a feast we're going to have... rabbit sushi! How...perfectly nasty. Well...it beats the alternative. I wonder if the dummy remembers that it has to be very small pieces.'

It was time consuming and somewhat disgusting eating for himself and feeding her. They could not afford to have a fire that could draw any attention, so they had to eat the meat raw. He also had to, again, cut the pieces of meat into something that he could handle with her limited capabilities.

He remembered that this friend who taught him the snares had also told him the difference between cottontails and jack rabbits. Most of the time, jack rabbits had worms. He was not sure whether these rabbits were closer to cottontails or jack rabbits. Before he could eat these Russian rabbits, he had to dig through their entrails looking for…anything that looked…in any way suspicious. He remembered back home having to gut a chicken. It was not as bad as gutting two rabbits. He had eaten the chicken – cooked. There was no such luxury here.

After what was the first of many nauseating meals he always threw the bones near the trunk of an evergreen with very low branches. He then packed up and headed out to put more distance between him and the crash site…still using an American toy to keep going in the right direction.

The scenery rarely changed. Most of the time, the land was rather barren. Nothing but white snow everywhere. In most cases it was blowing around because there seemed to be very little to stop the wind. When he could find forests of evergreens, it actually seemed warmer. The trees would block most of the wind and without wind it was always warmer…or at least it felt warmer.

He would scrape a notch on the side of the sled. He was using the notches to count the number of days he had been walking. He had no idea how far he was getting each day and he had no idea how far he had to go. He kept the compass on west by southwest for almost eleven days. Then he realized that that might not be such a good idea. That would take him to…(?) He changed his heading to southwest. He could not remember which country was where. Yugoslavia, Bulgaria, Romania, Czechoslovakia, Hungary…where was he headed? He knew that Poland and East Germany were the farthest north, but neither one was better or worse than any of the iron curtain countries. Was he going to get near the border of West

Germany? Austria? Greece? That brought up another country – Albania. What little he knew of Yugoslavia, Bulgaria or Romania – he knew even less about Albania. The possibilities were giving him a headache.

"*One Day at a Time*", became a song that he had heard and he sang to himself on several occasions. He could not think of many other songs that were appropriate to the situation. Songs from singing groups came to mind and he sang them as well, however, most of the singing just gave him a dry throat. Even though it dried his throat, the rhythm helped a little in the boring trudging along. It also took his mind off of the horror he would face...if caught.

He was not sure if he was getting stronger or the sled was getting lighter. Each time he had to change Marie's diaper he had discarded the soiled fabric. He had no way of cleaning anything so it could be disastrous to her health to reuse something. The bits and pieces of clothing that he was leaving behind could not possibly be that heavy that it would make the sled lighter...once discarded.

He trudged on. If it had not been for that stupid little toy compass he was not sure as to whether or not he would have tried at all. Of course he would have tried. He had no other choice. Run... or go to a gulag...or get executed.

One day when he had snared two rabbits, he was heading back to Marie and nearly lost control of his bodily functions when he came across a huge wolf. The beast lowered its head and growled at him. He could see the hair standing up on the back of the angry canine. What to do? What to do? He was drawing a complete blank. The wolf was obviously hungry and...he had not killed both rabbits...yet. He had tied one of them up. He threw the live rabbit towards the wolf. The wolf backed up snarling fiercely, at first. It looked down and saw the struggling rabbit. It slowly walked up to the rabbit and sniffed. It looked up at Bradley and he could not tell what was in its eyes. The wolf then grabbed the struggling rabbit and ran off. Bradley let out a long relieved sigh...and then checked his pants for any dampness.

He had heard that music would soothe or charm the savage breast. The breast of that beast was savage, however, it was just savage because of hunger. He was going to have to feed the wretched thing in order to soothe it and keep himself from becoming a buffet for the savage beast. He wondered how often he was going to have to feed a wolf.

Day after day he slogged on. Avoid, avoid, avoid, avoid, avoid, avoid...avoid people, avoid roads, avoid towns, avoid farms, avoid railroad tracks, avoid wild animals, avoid open areas, avoid... rivers!

Rivers! He came through a clump of evergreens. The only kind of a tree that gave him any kind of cover. He sat down panting. He stared in total despondency. He was looking across a river that was wider than any creek, stream, river or lake that he had seen in central Georgia. He looked to the north – there was a large community of some kind off in that direction. It was night time so all he could see was a large group of lights. He looked to the south – just mainly wild woodland. Not much of a choice.

He had to avoid people because he had no idea who might be KGB. He had heard that the KGB were usually identifiable because they were the ones who were dressed better. There was always that danger of finding one of them...among humans. South it is. He headed south away from the community. He needed to find a narrower part of the river (if there was that sort of area) in order to cross. Maybe, hopefully, by the grace of God, the river would take a westerly track and he would not have to worry about crossing it... yet.

He kept close track of the compass. As he followed the river south, it was going slightly to the south-southwest. After what seemed several hours, to him, the river snaked backwards to the southeast. There was no way to change the subject, even in his own mind. Eventually he was going to have to cross this monstrous obstacle.

He continued south trying to see if there was anything that could help. Could he find a log or something that he could use? Was he going to have to manufacture his own dugout canoe? Could he find a boat that he could steal, without raising too much alarm? Could he find some shallows?

He finally came upon a small pier. There were four rowboats tied up on the south side of the pier. Okay, there are some boats. They look sturdy. They looked cared for. They belong to somebody. He decided that the best thing to do was look around a little longer... maybe another day. Then, under the dark of night he would commit grand theft...rowboat. After what the Russians wanted to charge him with, what possible difference would it make if he stole a lousy rowboat?

While waiting, he set out some snares. He could not believe how lucky that he had been so far with catching rabbits. They were abundant throughout all of the countryside that he had covered so far. As he was setting the fourth snare he heard the familiar snap as one of the snares had snagged something. He clubbed the rabbit, removed the snares and headed back. We have tonight's dinner and the bait was too precious to leave behind for any reason.

As he gutted the rabbit he told Marie what he was thinking of doing. Again she started moving her lips as if trying to say something but she could not seem to form words with her lips. He cut the rabbit up and started the time consuming feeding of Marie.

She mentally scoffed. Now, in order to prolong the torture, bone-brain Bradley is going to steal a rowboat...and try to get across...which ever river we're sitting next to. Maybe I'll get lucky, I'll fall off...with the sled and just drown. Maybe we'll both get lucky and drown...in the freezing water. I hope it ain't too painful.' She took as deep a breath as possible. 'I wouldn't be able to swim out of it anyway...now. Okay, great and mighty warrior, see what you can do...without killing both of us. This should be a real hoot.'

After finishing off the rabbit, he continued with the evening ritual of the hygienic cleaning of his patient. He started noticing that there were some kind of nasty looking marks on her back. He sighed. Bed sores were inevitable. He decided that the only way to fight that was to figure out some way to prop her up on her side in the sled.

While he was manipulating her positioning on the sled, he heard someone...singing. He could not understand any of the words and it did not seem to have a beat. He crawled back towards the pier. A man was in a rowboat, heading in the general direction of the pier, singing loudly. Every now and then he would stop singing and either belch or take a drink out of a bottle. He appeared to be *very* drunk.

Bradley's heart started hammering in his chest. Could he possibly be that lucky...again? At first he was going to wait and see what the drunk was going to do. Then he thought of Marie. He hurried back to the camp. He quickly packed everything in order to be ready...if he was going to get lucky on his first major river crossing. He did not want to leave anything behind. Going back for it would be a nightmare.

He pulled the sled back to his vantage point of overlooking the pier. He had not heard the drunk singing for a few minutes. He found out why all was silent – the drunk had passed out on the pier. He was laying, face down, near his boat. He was so drunk that he had done a rather sloppy job of securing the boat.

He looked up to the darkening night sky. "Hey God, is this you doing something for me? If it is, I think that I might be believing in you a little more."

He did not feel like going back and forth. He dragged the sled down with him as he slowly crept closer to the drunk. The man was face down on the pier and breathing regularly between occasional belches.

As he reached the pier the man suddenly convulsed. Bradley froze waiting to see what would happen. It did not take long. The man did not wake up as he spewed a huge fountain of vomit. Bradley had to close his eyes and try to block the sound in order to keep from losing his own dinner. When the noise ended, he opened his eyes. The man was still in the same position he had been before. He had lost all of the contents of his stomach and had not moved anything else or awakened.

Bradley had to move past the man (on the clean side of the pier) in order to get to the boat. He had to fight his own wave of sickness as he went by. The smell was horrid…even in the cold. He could not imagine what that man had eaten…or why. He tried to think of anything else to get his mind off of the repugnant mess on the pier.

The boat was not as big as he would have hoped for, but he was not going to be picky. He got hold of the line that had been loosely hooked up to a metal ring that was screwed into the pier. He secured it as best as he could while thinking of how he was going to get the sled in the boat without dunking Marie and himself. He brought the boat up to the pier sideways. Maybe that would help.

He noticed that there were some kind of packages in the boat as well. No time to check them out right now – he had to get the sled in the boat and get moving. Take the boat and run before anyone comes looking for the sleeping drunk. Avoid another possible disaster.

He did a quick check on all of the other boats tied to the pier and was able to obtain several coils of different types of rope. It would add to the burden on the sled, however, any new equipment was not going to be turned down. Any of these ropes could be a new snare or they could be used for…the possibilities were endless.

As he fought the heavy sled he would look back and check

on the drunk. Hopefully the man would not wake up for some time. He finally got the sled positioned in what appeared to be the most secure place it could be in the small boat. He pulled the rope away from the metal ring, set the oars in place, pushed away from the pier and started rowing hard for the other side.

'Incredible,' she thought. 'He actually managed to get this infernal sled on the boat without getting me dunked. I wonder how he could possibly be getting so lucky...or is he hiding the fact that... NAH! He's a lucky bumbler. I've heard that God watches out for fools and the innocent...I wonder if...NAH! Dumb luck!'

He found that he was not really ready for this kind of exercise. After just a few minutes his shoulders were really hurting. From the shore, this river had not looked this wide. He tried to think of anything he could do in order to get the task done more efficiently. He remembered a few things about using the legs. He started pushing more with his legs and he could feel the boat moving faster with less pain in his shoulders and back. So there is something to using the legs instead of trying to use just the arms.

He would stop rowing every ten strokes and listen for engine noised. He had seen numerous barges going about their business during the day. Now that he was out in the middle of the river – without any light – he had to watch out for them because they could not see him...because they were probably not looking for any escaping enemy agents.

He heard the noise that he was dreading the most. It was coming from his left. He turned and saw some lights on the sides of the barge as it chugged along. He figured that there was no way to get past it before it got to him. He quickly turned back. Four strong, desperate pulls on the oars and then let it drift. He did not see anyone on the deck as it went by. They probably had enough sense to stay inside where it was warm.

Then he got hit by the wake. He nearly panicked as the little boat rocked violently in the waves. He could hear water slopping into the boat as he held on to the boat and the sled. When the rocking finally calmed, he let out a long sigh. He lightly tapped his feet in the bottom of the boat listening for any splashing. He heard nothing new, so somehow, the little boat had not taken on any water in the rocking.

Then he noticed that the boat was spinning slightly. He nearly panicked…again. Which way was he supposed to be going? He had no idea how much of a turn had occurred. Which way was the bow pointing? Then he slapped himself in the head – he still had the compass. He breathed a long sigh, pulled out the compass, got his bearings, used the oars to get the proper heading and then rowed for all he was worth. He prayed that he could get to the other side before another barge came along.

'Well you got lucky again,' she thought. 'Even I could hear that barge. Amazing how big the waves. Once again, I don't understand how he can be so lucky.' She tried to look over at him. 'Or maybe…I didn't get a rookie…and…he's hidden his real capabilities…until it really counts.' She wondered who the real Patsy was.

He counted as he rowed. Every fifteen pulls he would stop, listen and check the compass…again. It seemed to be getting even darker and there was only a crescent moon. He wished that the compass had been the type that glowed in the dark but hey – you can't have everything that you want – or need...just thank God for what you do have.

He rowed, for what seemed hours of torture. He suddenly came to an instant surprising halt and heard a loud scraping sound. He looked behind him and he saw a snow covered shoreline with leafless trees. He sat there panting heavily. He was a little too tired to rejoice over the fact that he had finally made it. Plus, now, he had to think of a way of getting Marie out of the boat...again...without dunking her.

'Okay, now what?' She tried to look either direction and see what was going on. 'He actually found the other side...if it IS the other side. Ain't no pier here, Mister Bone-Brain? What are you planning on now? If you're going to dunk me...please slit my throat first. I'd rather die from blood loss than freezing to death while drowning. Of course I...really don't know which one would be more merciful...or faster.'

When he finally got sufficient strength back, he moved to where he was leaning forward over the bow. He used an oar to check the depth. He laughed from the relief as the oar almost instantly hit bottom. He moved it around a little in order to assure himself that he had not just got stuck on a big rock. The boat had stopped on something...what? He slowly crawled around the boat and found the culprit boulder on the port side of the boat. He pushed away from the boulder and he used the oar, pushing against the bottom, to get himself closer to the bank. Every inch helped.

The white snow could easily be seen against the darkness of the river. It helped immensely in being able to get as close to the shore as possible. When the pushing against the bottom did not get him any closer to the shore he decided it was time to get out. He again checked the depth with the oar, between the boat and the bank…inches! It was less than two feet to the bank. He was not sure how waterproof these boots were and he did not want to find out the hard way. His feet might have been in the water for…how long?

He laid on his back for a few moments and rested before preparing for the next move. He felt himself nodding off and realized that he did not have time to sleep right now. To get this far and be found asleep in a stolen boat…not good.

He splashed his face with a little icy river water. It bit like fire and absolutely shocked him awake. He shook his head and dried his face as quickly as he could. He stood up, found the bow line and threw it to the shore. He felt that the boat was (hopefully) secure enough for him to take the step from boat to bank…it was.

He looked around and did not see any form of pathway or walkway near him. He pulled the on the line. He had to fight to get all of the tonnage of the boat, sled, Marie and whatever else was in the boat up on the shore. Once he had the boat up there, he pulled the sled off of the boat and saw that she was awake.

"We made it," he panted quietly. "God alone knows how, but we're on the other side…of this lousy river."

One blink. 'Yeah, God alone knows. I certainly don't put that much hope in you and your abilities…unless you *did* keep something hidden from me. As much as you fought against me, you could have hidden…anything.'

He was ready to push the boat out into the water when he

remembered the packages. He sighed. He pulled the three packages out. They were just bundles. One bundle contained two loaves of that dark bread and four of, what appeared to be, some kind of turnip. Another bundle contained – what he estimated – a six pound wheel of cheese. The third bundle had three carefully wrapped liter bottles of vodka (big surprise).

He looked up to heaven. "For what we are about to receive, we are grateful. Boy, are we *extremely* grateful."

He placed the oars back in the boat and pushed it out as hard as he could. He watched for a few moments as the slow current finally took it away into the darkness.

He then made a meal for the two of them. They polished off one entire loaf of bread, one turnip and about one fourth of the cheese. It had been some time since his stomach had been that full... of something other than raw rabbit.

Marie just looked at him with a blank expression. She did not seem to be able to show any emotion. He wondered just how much brain damage she had suffered.

'Got lucky again, didn't you,' she thought facetiously. 'Bread, cheese and turnips.' She sighed mentally. 'Beats the tar out of the other menu.'

"Do you want to eat any more right now?"

Two blinks. 'Save it for later...just before we get captured, dummy. Then it'll be evidence that they can use against you for stealing a boat.'

"Okay. I'll get us away from the bank into some trees over

there and we'll hide there for the rest of the night."

One blink. 'Good idea, dummy. Hide…what a concept?'

She had plenty of time to contemplate the events that had occurred in that interrogation room…where she had been strip-searched. They said that the contacts had confessed. 'That is impossible. They would have to have had people watching that public bathroom…all day…the next day. Ludmilla wasn't supposed to go in there…until after she got off work…the next day. She wouldn't have exchanged the bra…until then. They would have to watch that one stall…all day…and Ludmilla would rather die than give up anything. Maybe I should have said something to confuse them…at that time…like…oh say…you mean that all fourteen of my contacts confessed? That would have sent them on a real wild goose chase…since I only have three contacts in Moscow. No, that wouldn't have been too good an idea. If we hadn't gotten away, they would have tried to torture the information out of me…and what should I have said? Maybe some silly nonsensical comment from a spy novel?'

He lost track of how many days he had been traveling. Carving notches was time consuming and it was dulling the knife. He could not think of any other way of keeping track of time and he was not sure whether it was necessary or not. At first it had seemed interesting – now it seemed redundant – as well as time consuming. Scratching the sled with the knife also made some rather unnecessary noise.

He had considered the possibility of asking her to keep track of the days...how? She had no capability of feeding herself, she had no capability of hygiene, so just what could she do in order to keep track...of anything? All she could have done was keep track of it in her head. That might keep her mentally alert...would that really help him?

The only thing that she was good for – at the moment and in her condition – was sharing warmth, when he rested or slept. She did not seem to be getting any better. She still could not move very much or speak. It was frustrating having nothing but – what seemed to be – one-way conversations.

Several times she had moved her lips as if to try to say something, but whatever it was, communication was difficult. He could sit there asking yes/no questions forever until he hit on the subject and he just did not have the time, or the patience. He had to keep moving, whenever he had the strength to continue. Lollygagging in any one area for an extended length of time was totally counterproductive.

One evening, before he was able to set up the snares and catch their late meal, as he was hiding her and the sled under a large evergreen, he heard the sounds of several vehicles driving towards him. He jumped down under the tree with her and looked out trying to see who and what was driving around in this area...where there were no roads.

He shoved his hand into his mouth to keep from screaming. It was a military convoy of some type and they were driving track vehicles out here…in the wild. It was probably some kind of a military war game or practice maneuver.

He watched as he counted nine vehicles drive by the tree… and then stop…and cut their engines off. His entire body went limp as he observed them getting ready to bed down for the night…as well.

'Why…of all places…did you have to stop here?' he thought. 'Why couldn't you have gone…another five or six…or a thousand miles from here?'

Marie heard the vehicles and prepared herself for anything and everything possible to happen that was bad. A military convoy, out on practice patrols, just happens to stop here. 'I wonder if Bone-Brain Bradley will be able to get us out of this mess,' she wondered. 'Has his luck finally run out? Maybe it has. Let's just see what happens. All he has to do is remain silent, like me.'

The only thing that he could do that night was change her diaper, slowly and carefully, and then bed down as well…hungry. They would be hungry in the morning as well… if they were lucky enough to not be seen by any of the Russians. If he could remain as motionless as possible and hoped that he did not snore, they just might not be noticed at all. He listened for snoring as he was laying there and was relieved by the fact that there were plenty of the Russians who were noisy enough to cover any sounds that he might make.

While they were there, several of the Russians came up to their tree and left a deposit of their own on the branches, as they did their constitutionals for the night. Fortunately for the two people hidden under the branches, most of the liquids did not come anywhere near their exact spot, otherwise he would have to change more than Marie's diaper, after the Russians departed.

She listened to the conversations that she could hear. Any information that she could pick up might be useful – if she could communicate it to Bradley. From what she could hear, this convoy had nothing to do with the fugitive pair. She heard nothing but drivel about some soccer game and a few things about how cold it was. The men who were doing most of the talking did not want to be here, however, they were. It was just the enlisted personnel who were complaining. None of the officers were close enough for her to hear anything from them. She did not hear a thing that could be of any use to her plight.

The next morning, the tree once again received several bouts of golden baptisms. The men in the convoy made their breakfast and then were on their way.

Bradley waited until he could hear no more engine sounds before coming out from under the low branches. Now, he finally had the opportunity to set the snares for rabbits – and hope that there were still some in the area. He was ravenous and he was rather certain that she was in the same condition.

He searched the area to see if there was anything that might have been left behind by accident. The search was in vain. The Russians had left nothing useful behind. There were a few smoldering campfires, a lot of footprints and track marks from the vehicles. He had to go back to the tree totally irritated because of the fruitless search.

After the normal diaper change and taking care of his own bodily needs, he checked the snares and was relieved to find one rabbit. There was nothing wasted with that rabbit. They had still lost almost an entire day because of the extenuating circumstances.

He wondered about staying here for another day to recover from the shock and fear that they had gone through because of the Russian military exercise. He changed his mind when he figured that any rabbit population had been depleted in that area by the Russians.

She was still amazed, again, at how they had been able to dodge another bullet – especially one that big. She was becoming even more suspicious as to what he was capable of. It could not possibly be all luck – could it?

He trudged on. He kept the compass heading as close to west southwest as he could. He did not like the idea of trying to make an attempt at crossing over into Turkey. He did not know very much about the country, however, he was not sure how some Bedouin tribes might treat him, or her, or if they still had that type of people in Turkey any more.

He knew that this would probably lead him away from Greece, as well, but that would also avoid Albania – wherever that is. He had heard so much about all of these different countries – but Albania was a total mystery. He was also completely ignorant of a lot of the geography of Europe, especially the eastern part. Some of that stuff in school would sure help right now. You never know what you ignored in school could come back and haunt you. He remembered the names of several countries that were there, however, the exact locations eluded him – other than East Germany, Poland and Czechoslovakia.

They turnips had not lasted long, neither had the cheese. They ate most of the bread but he had saved several pieces of it as bait for the rabbits. He wished there had been more food in those packages. He had to shake his head and just think of how nice it had been to obtain what he had. The only thing he still had plenty of was the vodka. It came in handy for him to use as an antiseptic for cleaning Marie's bed sores as well as doing a little hygienic wiping whenever he changed her diaper.

Numerous times during the trip he would stop and look behind him. Were they following? Had they found the crash site? He knew, by now, they had to have been searching. That little convoy had never reached that unknown horror of a destination they were bound for. The people who had been in the vehicles were going to be missed. Had the snow covered every trace of their tracks from the crash site? He was not sure what to make of the situation. There were too many questions – and he was in no position to get any answers.

On and on he went. Back to one nasty raw rabbit after another. There were at least three occasions when he had to sacrifice a rabbit to another hungry wolf. He did not know how much longer his luck would continue. He had heard all kinds of horror stories about rabies running rampant in the wild animals of Russia. The only wolves he had run across were not foaming at the mouth and were happy to run off with their easily obtained meal. He remembered stories from back home about some rabid animals. Most of the victims of rabies had been raccoons, skunks and opossums. He wondered if there were any type of animal like that anywhere in Asia – or Eastern Europe – or wherever the heck he was.

Occasionally there was a fence…that separated one snow covered field from another snow covered field. He wondered what kind of crops they grew here and why the needed these flimsy fences. Maybe they were just boundaries between one crop and another. He did not really care that much, however, it did keep his mind busy and away from the total boredom of just walking.

He had seen very few other types of animals. He knew that the hat he was wearing was called *sable* fur. What is a sable? The only time that he had heard the term, it was in conjunction with something Russian. Apparently it was an animal that was indigenous only to this part of the world. Whatever it is it sure has a thick, warm fur.

He wondered if there were any wild bears in the area. He knew that the grizzly bear would eat anything. Are Russian bears the same? How big do they get? Do they hibernate? Some things that he might look up in some reference book in a library – if he ever got the chance to do anything like that again.

What other kinds of animals are there out here…running around in Russia…if he was still in Russia? He could remember all of the different types of critters that he had seen running around back in Georgia. Rabbits, squirrels, opossums, raccoons, skunks and the occasional stray dog or cat. He just did not understand what kind of animal would normally live in an environment like this cold Russian wasteland.

He came across several other rivers. None were as wide as that first one. Most of them were frozen over with thick ice and by crawling on his stomach and spreading his weight out as much as possible he had been able to get across with his passenger, dry and intact.

One river had been very low and he had been able to cross it in rocky areas where the water did not come above the soles of the boots he had stolen from the guards. It had been a royal pain getting the sled over the rocks, however, he had accomplished the tiresome task...finally.

He could not remember any rivers in Eastern Europe or Russia except the Volga and the Danube. He just hoped if he did come across the Danube that he was on the other side by then. That river was supposed to be really wide...from the stories that he had heard about it.

The first few days he had tried to shave with a bayonet. After a week of razor burn and another thing that dulled the knife, he gave up on that. He was getting a very full beard now. Yes he had been moving on this trip for quite some time.

He sat there cutting a rabbit and feeding the pieces to Marie. After the feeding he checked her for cleaning. He noticed that her stomach appeared to be a little swollen. What could have cause that? Then he remembered: Vitamin B deficiency! The main sign of this deficiency – that he could recall – was a distended stomach. Now she has a vitamin problem as well – great! Just what he needed, another problem. Each feeding after this he tried to get more into her in order to fight the deficiency. She ate everything he offered without hesitation or any form of argument. She was getting plenty to eat, but her body was not getting enough of what she really needed right now. He had no idea what would be a good source of Vitamin B. Predator animals are supposed to get all of their vitamins and other nutrients from the animals that they eat. Why is she getting insufficient nutrition from these rabbits? Are they all suffering from a vitamin deficiency as well? Now, he understood why you were supposed to eat a wide variety of foods, in order to obtain all of the nutrients that you really need. Variety makes a huge difference. He noticed that his belt was not getting tighter. Maybe it was her metabolism that just burned the B a lot faster than he did.

The next large river he came across, he wondered if he would be able to find another boat. He was not so lucky this time. He shrugged and headed north. He was going to check for anything or any way of crossing.

He saw a large train trestle in the distance. At first he was ready to give up and turn back the other way. Then he saw a man on the other side who walked across the trestle. He was not challenged at all. Where were the Russian guards? They had been stationed on one end of all of the trestles that he had seen earlier. They had stopped any traveler and checked their papers. There was no guard shack on this trestle – on either end. There was no guard. Why? Where was he?

He went back to Marie and told her about this anomaly. She just stared back at him.

"Do you think that was something that happens in Russia... only?"

One blink. 'Good an explanation as any, dummy. What's your plan now? Are you going to cross the trestle or swim? Maybe just sit down and cry about it – how about that?'

"Do you think that we're still in Russia?"

Two blinks. 'No, you idiot...by now we should be in Madrid. Maybe were in the Canary Islands! Keep walking and we should reach Newfoundland by noon tomorrow! A couple of days later we'll be able to sing *Deep in the Heart of Texas*!'

He looked back at the trestle. He wondered. 'Okay, I got out of Russia. What country am I in now? Apparently they don't care who crosses a trestle here...wherever *here* is.'

He looked as far as he could see in each direction on the railroad track. He had seen that the roads in Russia had towers with cameras on them, keeping track of who was on every meter of road in their jurisdiction. He had expected to see cameras on the rails as well. There were none here. This was very relieving...even though it was still confusing.

He decided to wait until dark to cross the trestle anyway because he did not want to get near any other human being. He had no idea what he would find but he did not want any nasty surprises. If he was going to be recaptured he wanted to put it off for as long as was humanely possible.

Maybe get lucky and catch a rabbit or two before the crossing. Eat it – or them on the other side of the river.

As the sun went down, he started creeping closer to the trestle. He strained his ears to hear anything man made. A cart, a train or an automobile. Anything where a human being would be involved.

It was completely dark when he finally left the cover of the trees. He heard a few birds. The thought occurred to him about how much easier it would be if he was a bird right now. Totally carefree in regards to the political system surrounding them. Just sit there and join in on the unwritten symphony. He also wondered about what kind of bird would be stupid enough to stay in this wintry wasteland and not migrate to…a place that was a lot warmer. Also, what kind of bird stays here in the cold and chirps all night? Maybe it was a female bellyaching at the male as to why they had not migrated with the others…before it got too cold to fly all that way.

He heard a train. He retreated back to the tree line close to the track. He snickered as it got closer. The communists used old fashioned, smoke belching locomotive engines behind the iron curtain. If a train was headed to the other side of the line, they would use a big modern diesel engine. Such hypocrisy. "Just like the hypocrite that sucked Sergeant Bradley F. Dooley into a mysterious mission behind communist lines, without letting him know anything of what was going on," he muttered in disgust. "Untrained, unwitting and ignorant…and now unable to figure out what to do next…until something happens."

After the train had gone by he headed up to the tracks as quickly as he could and started to cross on the trestle. He suddenly re-discovered that the sled was not going to cooperate on anything but ice or snow. He had to use an inordinate amount of strength dragging the, suddenly, very heavy sled across the wooden trestle. The scraping noise that it make while crossing the bridge was almost deafening. It seemed to take forever. When he finally got to the other side, he found snow at the earliest possible opportunity and headed for it.

He looked back at the trail that he had left in the snow. He noticed that there were several trails in the snow from...what? Possibly wolf tracks, or some other canine. There were tracks that looked like something from a deer. There were lots of rabbit tracks.

Then he noticed that there were other tracks from large sleighs, horse hooves, human tracks and a few birds. He again wondered what kind of bird would stick around in the snow. He did not have time to wonder very long. He had not seen many humans in the area, however, the tracks here were abundant. All of them heading to the trestle. Apparently, the trestle was very commonly used in this area – by any and every creature in the area that could not fly.

He pulled the compass out, got his heading and started pulling. He took about ten steps and stopped. Dragging the sled over the trestle where there was no snow had sapped his strength badly. Wonderful night – he had achieved only one quarter of a mile and he was exhausted. At this rate, it would be summer before he got to...where *ever*.

He set his snares in an isolated area where he saw rabbit tracks. He made sure that it was away from any human tracks. He went back to the sled. After snuggling close to Marie for warmth he fell asleep. Falling asleep was no problem in this case.

He awoke the next morning, more rested than he had been for some time. He checked the snares and was rewarded with three rabbits. After doing some of the daily rituals of eating raw rabbit and changing Marie's diaper, he checked the compass and headed out.

Marie, again, was wondering how long their luck could possibly last. A boat, frozen rivers and a train trestle. She was wondering why she had never had that kind of luck. She had always had to rely on her training in order to get out of situations. Here she was now with a dummy who just seemed to stumble onto good fortune and get out of sticky situations by total dumb luck. 'The world is not fair,' she thought.

One day he was walking along among the trees when he came across a fox. He did not think much of it at first because he figured that the foxes were usually the type to run from humans. He had heard of the British Fox Hunts where they had to chase one of the little beasts for miles. He continued walking.

A few moments later he saw a movement off to his right. He looked quickly in that direction and his blood froze. It was the fox. This time, however, he took a closer look at the little beast – particularly the mouth. Frothy foam was all around the mouth. You do not need to be a professional veterinarian in order make that diagnosis.

He had thought about the possibility before. A rabid animal. Everything he knew about them was that a fox is normally a nocturnal creature. Seeing one out during the day was a warning that there was something very wrong. Seeing its frothing mouth and hearing it growl made him very worried.

He shrugged the sled harness off of his shoulders. He slowly went back to the sled, reached down and pulled one of the rifles out. He brought it up and aimed it. He was terrified of risking a gunshot. He was equally terrified of the diseased menace that was creeping dangerously closer. He re-aimed the rifle, not quite sure what to do, but he knew that he could not let this sinister little thing get too close.

The fox suddenly lurched forward and Bradley pushed the barrel of the rifle out at the snarling thing. The fox caught the barrel in its mouth and bit down. Bradley flinched, pulled back and accidentally pulled the trigger. The bullet ripped through the throat and removed a large portion of the spinal column, spraying a bloody mess all over the snow. The shredded remains lay in the reddened snow, going through a few final death twitches. He stood there paralyzed with fear for several moments as he looked over the gory scene in front of him. He did not move until the fox finished all of the twitching. He staggered away from the mess, checking his crotch for any unwanted moisture.

He was amazed at how the shot had been somewhat "muffled" as it went off in the animal's throat. That had been extremely lucky for him. He also considered himself very lucky that this was the first rabid animal that he had run into on this quest.

He spent three hours cleaning the barrel of the rifle. He used quite a bit of snow wiping it down. The gloves that he had been wearing at the time were definitely going to be left behind. He was not going to take any chances.

While cleaning the rifle, he stopped every few moments and listened for any new sounds. Nothing – thank God. It was amazing how birds could be so easily startled by unusual sounds, but go back to their normal routine, so easily and quickly.

He came to an area that was a little frustrating. It was getting late and he could see a line of lights that extended in both directions as far as he could see. He found a good place to hide Marie and went down closer to check on this line of lights.

He crept up under a large evergreen and looked towards the line. He pulled out the binoculars and scanned the area. Approximately ten feet from his hideout, was a road. On the other side of the road was a large open field. Also on the other side was a row of tall guard towers, about 100 yards apart. On the far side of the field was a barb-wired fence. On the other side of the fence, there was a lot of trees…and a pole. It was about four feet high and it stood out like a beacon…on the other side of the fence.

He was ready to shout with delight. He had reached the border. He did not know whether he was in Czechoslovakia or East Germany, however, he did know that it was West Germany on the other side of that fence. When he had first entered the country, they had given him a welcome and warning briefing. They had showed a picture of one of those poles. The poles were striped like a barber pole, but they were the colors of the West German flag – black, red and yellow. The West Germans had placed those poles, every 100 meters along the border between West Germany and their iron curtain neighbors, East Germany and Czechoslovakia. In the briefing, they had been told that they should not get near those poles. All American military personnel were forbidden from getting within ten kilometers of the communist borders. If you were out walking along in the countryside and you saw one of those poles, you turn around "with all haste" heading west and get away from the communist border.

Very few Americans were allowed near the border and only under the strictest of conditions, on official business only...or if you happened to be part of some silly tourist thing that showed you a fence...that bordered a communist country.

They definitely stood out against the normal vegetation of the area. The poles were a beacon of freedom. A beacon that now seemed to mock him as it stood there – on the other side. He could see it. He dare not approach it. The guards would see him and shoot. Even if they were asleep and did not see him the field was full of anti-personnel land mines. The fence was electrified. His elation turned to gloom and he slinked his way back to Marie.

She was grateful for the body heat. Alone she was not putting out that much. True, with all of the coats and rubber she was heavily insulated against the cold. The real warmth, however, came when he was next to her. 'Now here is the story – we're close to the border. Right! We somehow made it across Russia, Poland and Czechoslovakia...or East Germany and now, we're staring at the fence...on the other side of a minefield...with a collection of guard towers...armed with large, fully automatic guns. We might as well still be just outside of Moscow. Who does he think he's kidding? Go get a rabbit, dummy. I'm hungry!'

10

Bates looked at the report in front of him and was thoroughly confused as to why he had not heard anything more about Wintergreen…plus one. There had been several more reports about agents, from other western nations, that had been caught or killed. The only thing on Wintergreen – caught…and then disappeared off of the face of the earth. She disappeared along with…Patsy.

Once the fraud had been exposed and the USA leaked it to all allies, all nations recalled their agents…what few they could get back. It was very difficult for a lot of them because they were already being followed by the KGB as soon as they entered the country and now a lot of their contacts were being exposed as well. The ruse by the Russians had demolished a great number of spy rings that had taken years to set up.

Another thing that had surprised Bates was the fact that it was the contacts of Wintergreen who had sent the valid, unimpeachable information about this new technology being a total fraud. Somehow, she had made contact with them, they knew about the fraud and they had reported it to the west…but she was still captured – and now - thundering silence. The Russian propaganda machines should be pouring salt in every wound and orifice of the United States, gouging in every way that they could…but nothing.

He went back to the old report. According to that one, 44021 and 98174 were being transferred to "Area 5". What is Area 5? Where is Area 5? He had no way of contacting anyone inside the iron curtain to find out. Virtually all of the contacts had been depleted. If it was a place where they could torture or drug an agent into confessing...apparently Wintergreen was tougher than he thought or she was dead. If Dooley had been taken to this facility... he had nothing that he could tell them. He was not an agent so he had nothing to tell. If they did not believe that he was not an agent, which was the truth, they would torture him or drug him until he was a mental vegetable...or totally insane...or dead. The possibilities were endless and infuriating.

The Russian propaganda machines were silent...why? Were they waiting until they had something that was really juicy before they...? At least there was nothing about the missing Wintergreen... plus one...at the moment. There were a few other things that had come out about all of the ones they had captured...nothing else. One report after another came in from information, on many subjects, gleaned from the other side, however, there was still nothing to go on as to what had happened to his third agent...plus one.

The silence from the east was very confusing. The propagandists were constantly milking the capture or killing of all of the ones that they had found. The poor, innocent, happy, fun-loving people of the Soviet Union were being plagued by the greedy, imperialistic, decadent pigs of the west, with all of the spies and saboteurs that had been uncovered by the superior technology of the Soviet Union. The KGB was doing its job of protecting the happy, fun-loving people of the east from the greedy, capitalistic monsters of the west.

He was getting headaches, wondering what had happened to the pair and when the law would come down on him, like a ton of bricks…make that several tons of law books. As long as no one found out about Dooley, Bates was safe. As soon as the Russian propagandists let it be known about this Air Force Sergeant…the possibilities here were aggravating.

Bates had spent twenty-seven years in the US Air Force, obtaining the rank of Colonel. He had been going for Brigadier General…and then one little blemish caught up with him and he had to settle for retiring as a Colonel. He had gone to the CIA and been able to rise up there, very rapidly, because of what he had done in the Air Force. Now, all of that seemed to be getting him nowhere, in regards to this mysterious disappearance and silence from Wintergreen…plus one. One little mistake that could flush everything he had worked for…down the toilet.

He shook his head. Might as well enjoy what he could for as long as he could and…cross the bridge of shame…when, or if it came to that. He had made the mistake of putting his real name on that marriage certificate and license. He hoped that he could spin it that he was doing it because it helped one of his agents with a cover and he could claim ignorance of the fact that Dooley was active duty US Military. All of the decisions that had to be made, right now, were just pure conjecture, considering that he had no idea where Dooley was or what he was doing…or if he was even still alive. He cleaned a few things out of the desk…just in case.

He was thinking of obtaining a copy of the *Posse Comitatus*, in order to find out what might happen. No, that would mean that he knew of the law and that he had knowingly sent a member of the US Military on a civilian mission. He snarled. All he could do was sit here on pins and needles. Just stew and fret and wonder when the axe would fall.

11

In the Russian KGB headquarters, there were several personnel who were just as frustrated as Bates. They had perpetrated a giant fraud against the west and the dividends were immense. They had broken up at least fifty different spy rings from at least twenty different countries. The reports given to the United Nations were very one-sided. They even blamed the west for starting the rumors just so that they could invade the Soviet Union with all kinds of spies and saboteurs.

They did have the irritation of the fact that several foreign agents had escaped, even though they were just millimeters away from being caught. Some of them had found a way to suddenly elude the personnel who were tailing them and then suddenly turned up on the other side of the borders in Austria, Greece, Iran or Turkey or even Finland…or even one who somehow crossed over into China and was able to make it all the way to Thailand before he resurfaced.

It was also irritating how many of them had preferred suicide to being captured. The amount of intelligence data that could have been obtained would have been a wonderful addition to their propaganda efforts. The primary satisfaction with the dead ones was the refusal to give the bodies back to the country or origin. Russia would take care of the bodies…in a furnace. Considering the fact that there were so many dead, they did not want to waste any more resources on shipping dead bodies all over the world.

Then there was the mystery of 44021 and 98174. They were

to be transported to Area 5, where they would have been questioned until they broke. So far, all of the foreign agents that had been a "guest" of Area 5 had been broken. These two, one professional and one beginner, were being transported there and had vanished off the face of the earth…along with their escorts. How does anyone just… vanish? During the winter, in Russia, it was possible for people to freeze to death and not be found until the spring thaw. The vast majority of those people were alone. This should not apply here. Those two had been in a warm vehicle with an escort. The vehicles, the spies and the escorts…all missing. How?

When someone was taken to Area 5, the route would vary, depending on who was in charge of the expedition. This way, no westerner could possibly come up with a rescue for their agents. They did not know which route had been taken and because there had been a huge winter squall, there had been a few landslides and avalanches in some of the mountainous areas. If they had been caught in one of these avalanches, they could be buried under tons of snow and well hidden until the spring thaw. Then they would have to search over twelve hundred kilometers of road, covering eighteen different routes to Area 5 and it would take an immense number of personnel to do it. Hopefully, the two American agents had been killed in the incident…if an incident had taken place. If not, by now, any tracks would be obliterated and once spring came…any trail would be colder than the winter itself.

Day after day, they listened for any information about a road that had finally been cleared of snow. Was there any evidence that the small convoy had been buried there? Was there any information about any wreckage in that area? Was there any information about any bodies in that area? The questions all remained unanswered.

If the American agents had been somehow rescued, that would be a major embarrassment as well. Losing them to an avalanche was one thing – hearing that they had been rescued would be inexcusable, unforgiveable…possibly a career ending mistake… for at least three KGB agents. The only thing that they would be able to recover any dignity from a successful rescue mission would be that they had murdered several Soviet citizens in committing this act and they could get all kinds of mileage on that propaganda.

Just like their American counterparts, they continued reading and re-reading numerous reports, trying to see if any of them rendered even the slightest bit of information as to what had happened.

One man came up with the idea of having helicopter patrols go out, however that was scrapped because they did not know which of the routes had been taken. Even if they did know which route… where did the convoy disappear? If the convoy was ambushed by some unknown American unit, by now the remnants of the action would be buried under snow. The helicopter personnel would be looking for suspicious lumps in the snow. How many of those could be found in the Russian countryside…in the dead of winter? What, exactly, constitutes a *suspicious* lump? They would have to go through the usual irritation of waiting for the spring thaw before they could find any evidence of where they were and what happened.

The main KGB agent in charge of this investigation kept on receiving reports on a man pulling a sled. He had to keep reminding those giving the reports that he was looking for a man and a woman. One man wearing a Soviet military uniform, pulling a sled was probably an enlisted man who was being punished for some act of insubordination. If the KGB were to start investigating every time an officer punished some unruly, disobedient or rebellious underling, the officers would not be able to do their job at all.

He kept digging through all of the reports, looking for a man and a woman. There had been several reports, however, each one turned out to be reports on someone who belonged in that area, or was authorized to be there. All couples that were investigated were not the pair he was looking for. Two couples had somehow got lost in a snowstorm. They had wandered into an area where they should not be, however, they were Soviet citizens and their stories were hard to debate. There had been a few places where blizzards had been fierce and no one was expected to be able to fully function in a blinding snowstorm. Those people had been returned to their rightful place and the episode was forgotten.

The frustration was unending…even the fact that frustration was becoming a much overused word.

12

She hated what was happening. She was being dragged on this accursed sled and there was nothing she could do about it. Her view of the world did not change at all, now that he had put that stupid little snow shield above her face. Even if she could move her head from side to side, in order to see something else, what was she going to see other than snow...or trees? Big deal! What else was there to see?

She wished that he would get it over with. 'Kill me,' she thought. 'Just kill me and I won't have to suffer any more of this... uselessness.' Then she remembered that as long as she was alive, he had someone to snuggle close to when it was really cold – like those blizzards. She remembered the blizzards. The good thing about them was that they wiped out any trail that the dummy might have left behind him. No one would be expected to follow another person in a blizzard. It would have been the same in a sandstorm – all traces completely wiped out.

He would talk to her and tell her about anything that had happened that was different that day. She did not buy any of his stories. Feed a wolf one of the rabbits so that we could survive? What utter nonsense. She had heard that story several times. She still did not believe it. She had read a report about the Russian army going out in helicopters, hunting down all wolves in an attempt at eradicating them from the countryside altogether. It had been an attempt at getting rid of a dangerous predator while also trying to get rid of, what they considered, the main contributor to rabies. She could not possibly believe that they had run across as many wolves as he claimed, unless the Russian military was totally incompetent.

A rabid fox? If he had fired a shot at the thing, why did she not hear the shot being fired? 'Oh…according to dummy, the barrel of the gun was in the mouth of the fox at the time. I'm supposed to believe that nonsense,' she thought. 'A rabid fox starts nursing on a gun barrel and he just happens to pull the trigger at that exact moment? I'll believe it when I see proof of it.'

Day after day of being dragged behind him in that sled. She was still amazed at his stamina when it came to walking. She had observed him on that track and she had never seen anyone who could walk that long without having to rest and/or soak their tired feet… in, at least, some hot water. He had gone on and on and did not look tired at all – just sweaty.

Wolves, birds and a rabid fox. 'Did he see anything else… other than that drunken fool that he got the turnips…and a boat from? Oh yeah, there was the military convoy.' There had been a few different types of deer that had been seen off in the distance, however, it would have been foolish taking a shot at one of them. That would have given away their position to anybody who could hear the shot.

Now a new story. After all the time that he had been dragging her across Russia, he now claimed that they were just on the other side of a minefield from the West German border. She found that completely impossible to believe. That meant that he had crossed through either Poland or Czechoslovakia – or just the entire length of Czechoslovakia. Or they had crossed Poland and were now in East Germany. His sense of direction would have to be uncanny in order to have pulled that one off. Yes, you can use the position of the sun to keep track of where you are going, however, he had gone on and on...sometimes at night and sometimes during the day. He would have probably been better off if he had headed northwest to Leningrad and made an attempt at crossing over into Finland. Maybe even a water crossing out of Riga. Right now, the snow would be very deep and it would be impossible for any of the Russians to chase him down in armpit deep snow.

He talked about that wooden pole that the West Germans had placed along the fences between East and West, all along the communist borders. She could not argue with that. She had seen a few pictures of those poles, however, actually being close enough to the fence to see one? She had never been there.

She was miserable because of the bed sores and diaper rash. Over and over in her mind she wished that he would just get it over with. 'Just do the cold sandwich and then I don't have anything to worry about and I won't be feeling any more pain.'

Lately he had been giving her more food. She could not understand why. If he was trying to fatten her up, it would have been far better for him to eat more of those rotten rabbits than to give the meat to her. She was equally confused over the fact that even though he was feeding her more, she still felt hungry afterward, than when they first started on this quest for the western frontier. She was not burning any calories just laying there...why was she needing more food? Something just did not seem right about her current dietary needs. She wondered if she were becoming a glutton. 'For rabbit sushi? Oh God forbid!'

Here he is again with more garbage about the fence. The fence is just on the other side of the minefield…that is just on the other side of the road. The only reason that she believed that there was a road nearby was because she did hear some vehicles driving by…that did seem very close to her position.

Time to wipe my butt and feed me more raw rabbit. 'Aren't there any other kind of rodents in this country? Why don't you go shoot a sable? I wonder what those things taste like. Of course, if we're no longer in Russia, I don't think that we'll see any sables in this area. Try finding a squirrel! No, that would be useless because they have very little meat on them and it wouldn't be worth the trouble.'

She tried to keep her mind busy thinking of what other animals might be in the wild in this area. All of the animals that she could think of were…somewhere else. Zoology had never been one of her favorite subjects. 'Why am I thinking about all of those things? I could be…' She grunted in frustration. 'What else do I have to do other than think…and crap my pants? Oh, yes, I think about eating more of that nasty raw rabbit meat.'

She began to wonder about the truth of being that close to the West German border. It had been several days since he had dragged her across the countryside…anywhere. The only time that he had stopped before, to stay in one place, was during a blizzard. There had not been a blizzard for several days, just mild snowfall. Maybe…by some gargantuan stroke of fool luck, they *were* near West Germany. So what! How was he supposed to get across the minefield and get over the electrified fence, with an invalid, without getting both of them shot?

13

He pulled the camp closer to the road. He felt he had to try to figure some way of circumventing the guards, the fence, the mines, the very well lit area, the truck patrols and...the dogs. Thankfully they did not seem too interested in anything on Bradley's side of the road. The only thing that he could think of was to observe and see if there was some kind of weakness in the system. Some kind of chink in their armor that he could exploit...with his helpless passenger.

For some reason the ground, in this area, was covered with more ice than snow. As a result, he left virtually no trail while pulling her down towards the road.

There was a very large clump of evergreens near the road. He pulled Marie into this clump, found a good hiding area in it, did his best to make her comfortable and started his own patrolling.

He spent several days observing the actions of the guards as they patrolled. They had very set schedules. They had very set patrol areas. Of course they would stick to them, when they were being constantly hounded by an autocratic hierarchy. If they did not, those same autocrats could ship them off to Siberia...for good.

One interesting thing that he noticed was that they had a dog patrol that walked very near the fence. He had been told that the open field on the "other" side of the fence was nothing but one big minefield. If the dog patrols were walking within a couple of feet of the fence, then there was obviously a clear area near the fence.

He wondered if he would ever be able to get close enough, safely, in order to utilize that knowledge.

The guards in the towers were changed four times a day. Two guards would climb up into the tower and get into position before the other guards would come down from the tower. They always did one tower at a time. That way, all towers were constantly manned and ready for any situation that could come up.

The lights were turned on before the sun went down and not turned off until the sun was already well up in the sky.

The dog patrols, he discovered, were inconsistent. The dog handler would slowly walk along the fence while another armed guard would follow closely behind. Bradley would do a slow count between each dog patrol and there was no consistency at all. Maybe they were just going out there to warm themselves up or warm up their dogs by moving around.

He could also see that the dog patrols had a very well-trod path up to the fence. They could make the (approximately) 100 yards from the towers to the fence with complete safety from the mines. They were, of course, being closely watched by the tower guards the whole time. Any attempt at bolting for the fence and suddenly you weight twice as much...because of a very large load of lead.

The truck patrols were very consistent. Shortly before the changing of the tower guards a truck would go by. Shortly after the changing of the tower guards a truck would go by. He seldom saw any other vehicles going by at all.

Other than the dog patrols he saw no other walking guards.

He felt very despondent over being an inmate in a place where the entire country was a prison.

Each day that he sat there, he had to go farther and farther in order to set up the snares. He was doing some major damage to the rabbit population in this immediate area. The bones that were piling up under the trees in this area were bound to bring groups of scavenging insects, once the weather warmed up. Every time he had his own bowel movement and a cleaning on her, that pile was getting larger as well. That was going to be on fantastically fertilized tree by the time this ordeal was over...no matter how it ended. When Spring time arrived, this area was going to be rather odiferous.

He finally ran out of diaper material. He had been using the thermal underwear and extra uniforms that he had stripped off of the guards at the crash site. He had been tearing it into any piece that he could use to diaper her. Now he was going to either have to start shredding coats – or use the sheets of rubber as diaper material. That stuff would be reusable. He wondered why he had not thought of that idea before.

He sat there watching everything going on with complete despair. The people who were manning the border were very determined to keep people inside. They kept people inside and constantly spouted propaganda that they were protecting the people behind the iron curtain from the decadence of the West. He wondered how many of the guards would jump the fence – if given the opportunity. What did it take to become one of those guards? How cold-blooded do you have to be? He did not really want to know.

He could see the fence, but could not go near it. He could

see that there was enough time to go between the dog patrols, if it were not for the guard towers. He could see the clear path to the fence but could not make it because of everything they had set up. They were definitely professionals in keeping people from obtaining freedom.

He slammed his fist into the ground in frustration. He had to shove his other hand into his mouth, in order to keep from shouting in pain. He looked at the ice where he had punched it – not a mark, not a sign that it had been struck in any way at all. He took out one of the bayonets and stabbed the ice hard. It did not puncture the ice very far at all.

He shook his head. Tunneling would be a very long and very impossible process. He had thought of some kind of haphazard tunnel. Why not? He had a compass. Once under the ground, he could keep his bearings with the compass. He looked at the heading on the compass as he stared at that pole on the west side. That pole that was striped with the three colors of the German flag, from top to bottom.

It was eight days in a row, where a fresh layer of snow fell during the night. During the day it would warm up a little, with a nice sunny sky. The sun would melt the top layer of snow (a little) and then freeze a new layer of ice during the night. He figured that since he could not break the ice here in the clump of trees – he would be able to crawl on his stomach (pulling the sled behind him) without breaking the ice between here and the fence. Use two or three of the big coats as cushioning, throw the rubber sheets over the coats, lift Marie over the fence, followed by the sled, followed by other supplies and then he would climb over. He would then pull all that cushioning and rubber over the fence with him, get packed up and then be on their way.

'Nice plan,' he thought. 'All I need is a long power failure, the guards in the towers to fall asleep and the dog handlers to forget their patrols. Easy – bull what?'

Eleven torturous days and nights he lay there looking at that pole and watching all of the guards on their rounds. He was beginning to get real despondent. He had hoped that Marie would have healed (at least to where she could talk) and then he would have been able to find out if she had a contact – somewhere near the border. He had hoped that somehow he could see a weakness in the ever-watching guards. Trucks, guards, dogs and lights: The guards of the prison were doing their job very well...of protecting the communist citizens from the decadence (and prosperity) of the evil west...and depriving him of getting home before...he tried to think. 'Did I miss Thanksgiving? Christmas? New Year's Day? What else have I missed?'

He wanted to go back to Marie and punch her in the mouth for getting him into this mess. If she had picked someone else or just left him alone, he would still be back there in West Germany, totally ignorant of any of this political intrigue and espionage. No, punching her out and maybe killing her would be too nice. If he had to suffer, so did she.

14

Bates was getting even more irritated and confused about the situation. Why have the Russians done nothing about this mess with Wintergreen...plus one? All of the information that they had intercepted said that 44021 and 98174 were to be taken to Area 5 for further questioning. Again, either they had not broken Wintergreen or they did not believe the patsy that she had with her and they were giving him no end of grief, attempting to get a different story out of him. What were they doing and why was there no new information about the two missing personnel?

Burke looked at Bates suspiciously. "You said that because of that Congressional Act, you're not allowed to use military personnel...without permission of the Secretary of Defense, right?"

"Right," said Bates calmly.

"So...why did you allow her to do it?"

"I didn't know that it was going to go this way. I thought that she would get in, get what she needed and get out. I had no idea that *anything* like this would happen. I never dreamed that...I just didn't think." He covered his face with his hands and growled.

Burke was still confused. "Why did Congress enact that legislation?"

Bates leaned back and sighed. "Because in the old west, some town Sheriff or Marshall would need a posse in order to go after some bad guy. Instead of forming a posse from the people of the town, a lot of them would go to a military fort and get the cavalry to go as the posse. Some of the troops were getting killed in these situations and in most situations, the troops were not performing their assigned patrols. Either way it was decided that the military should not be involved in civilian situations and *that* is why they passed the law."

"Has the Secretary of Defense ever given permission to anyone to use the military…on a civilian endeavor?"

"Not that I know of."

"Wait…if we're not allowed to use military personnel…why do we have you?"

"What do you mean by that?"

"You are a Colonel…in the United States Air Force. Did we have to get permission to use you in the CIA?"

Bates rolled his eyes. "I WAS a Colonel in the Air Force. I retired from the Air Force before I joined the CIA."

"Then why do you still go by Colonel?"

"Because I CAN! I achieved the rank and I can use it. The title is mine for life…now that I am no longer active duty. It doesn't carry the same power that it did when I was in the military, but I can still use the title."

"Okay, I'll buy that. I know that you were curious about Wintergreen. There are no new updates. The Russians still don't seem to be giving out any more information on her."

Bates shook his head. "What a pain!"

Burke looked at some of his paperwork. "We got a few bits of information from Wintergreen's connections. They said that they haven't heard anything about her at all. They got a few contacts of their own...in certain areas and no one seems to know anything."

Bates clenched his fists. "They can't have just disappeared... off the face of the earth."

Burke sighed. "There is another possibility. They were involved in a crash. The Russians don't even know where the crash is, and, no one will know anything until the Spring thaw. I remember a show on World War II. They said that when the snow melted from Leningrad...there were hundreds of bodies found...that no one knew about because they were all buried under the snow and frozen solid."

Bates nodded sadly. "If that happened...it still remains that we used a member of the United States military...without permission. Dead or alive, the results could still be the same...for us."

15

A Russian patrol had accidentally stumbled on the scene of the crash. The ill-fated convoy was found in the deep gully. A recovery team went there in order to determine what they might find in the wreckage. It took nearly four days to clear all of the snow away from the three vehicles. It was another day before all of the Russian personnel were accounted for at the crash site.

Now, the KGB were even more convinced that they were the ones who had been played for fools. This Dooley character may have been new, however, he was very clever because he had somehow caused this crash and the two spies had escaped. He was definitely someone that they had to find, break, and because of the murder of so many people, had to be executed for numerous crimes against Soviet citizens and the Soviet State. They would get all kinds of propaganda out of this one – once they recaptured him – if they could figure out which way the two fugitives went when they departed the scene.

Main problem: Find him and all accomplices. Did they head north in order to cross over to Finland or even as far north as Norway? Did they head southeast in order to cross the Caspian Sea to Iran? Did they go due south in order to cross the Caucasus Mountains into Iran or Turkey? Did they go due south to the Black Sea to cross over to Turkey? Did they head directly west in order to escape across the Baltic Sea from either Riga or Gdansk? Did they head across the frontier through Poland or Czechoslovakia or East

Germany, in order to cross into West Germany or Austria? Could they have gone south to cross through Romania and Bulgaria to get to Greece? The possibilities could drive a person insane unless they had some kind of good information.

The only thing that the Russians were sure of was that they would not have headed east. Too many obstacles in the way. The Ural Mountains, Afghanistan, the Himalayas, China, Mongolia, not to mention the sheer distance that they would have to go, even though one crafty individual had hopped a train and traveled the distance to China and had escaped.

Other KGB agents started checking on any sightings that had been seen in any of the directions that looked, in any way, questionable or feasible. They found two possible leads that had turned into nothing when the people involved could prove that they had a good reason to be where they were.

There were a few places between Moscow and Minsk where a single man had been seen pulling a sled behind him in the countryside. These were ignored because it was one man alone *and* they had said that he was in a Soviet military uniform. They needed a report with a man and a woman.

The reports of one man with a sled, in uniform, could not possibly have been what they were looking for. This Dooley had kept of the act of a tourist who was enraged over being treated like a spy. He was much too intelligent to dress like a member of the Soviet military and then brazenly walk around the countryside being weighed down by pulling a heavy sled. No, this had to be someone who was doing some kind of patrolling for some reason. If they did spot anything they were told to report it to one person. That agent was handling all of the information and would instruct them on which lead to follow.

The sightings of one man pulling a sled persisted from Minsk to Krakow in Poland. Again this was ignored because, again, it was just one person. Not to mention the fact that there was no possible way that any American could have walked that far. They were much too lazy and out of shape, to go through any kind of physical ordeal as long as a walking trek from Moscow to the West German border, through Poland and Czechoslovakia. It was utterly absurd.

The KGB started admonishing anyone who sent them a report of one person. It was stressed that they needed any unusual or unexplained sighting of a man with a woman. One man did not help, unless they could find him and prove who he was. If it was this Dooley character, then where was the woman? If she had died in the wreck, why did he take the body with him? How far could he have possible gone, dragging a dead body with him? If it was Dooley, that was this unexplained individual, he would have dumped the body and the sled long before he got to Poland. The bottom of a river that had since frozen over would leave them with no clues until Spring.

The KGB followed several more leads in Gdansk, Poland, one in Leningrad, two in Murmansk, several in Odessa...even one in Burgas, Bulgaria. All they did was, once again, confirm that these were people who were who they said they were and they were where they were authorized to be.

The frustration mounted as they could not find any information at all on the two fugitive spies. No matter what lead they had, all of them turned out to be nothing. The trail was totally cold and everything was guesswork as far as where these two conniving spies could be.

Of all the agents identified during the execution of the scam, this was the one and only situation where they had no final answer of what had happened to the spies involved. All others had escaped, been terminated or captured. Failure was not supposed to be an option. They had to solve this one, no matter what.

16

The wind picked up a little and bit right through him. He pulled the coat tighter around him. He guessed that Marie would be getting rather cold right now so it was time to huddle together.

He looked at the compass one more time. The needle would give him the heading…if he could ever find a way to get past all of the overkill guard systems that the communists had set up.

He went back to Marie. He did her necessary hygienic cleaning. He got the bedding ready and pulled her close.

He was irritated at the total lack of response on her part. Still no sign of healing at all. She still could not do anything for herself. She had virtually no control of any part of her body, except to be able to swallow small pieces of meat and blink her eyes.

The wind started blowing harder. Snow started coming down and swirling among the trees that they were hiding in. He tried to cover the two of them, even more, against the wind. In the entire time he had been trekking from somewhere in Russia, to…this place…wherever it was, he had not had to put up with very much really strong wind…for long. It had snowed several times during the journey and there had been a few white-out blizzards. One time it snowed for eight full days. He considered that he had been lucky that the wind had not been much of a factor. Lucky enough to get here and then get the door slammed in his face.

The wind started picking up even more. He could hear one

of the trees nearby creaking with the wind. Suddenly all of the snow on its branches fell on the tree that he was camped under. He huddled even closer to Marie. He was always listening for a protest of any kind from her…just in case she had healed to the point of being capable of speech. He never heard anything from her.

Approximately one hour later the wind was almost gale force. The wind was so hard that any snow that was flying around was not hitting the ground. The snow was flying parallel to the ground, as well as getting thicker…at least what he could see of it.

He tried to figure out a way to get the coats wrapped around a little better so that they would not blow away. The relentless wind was making it increasingly difficult even though the branches of the tree were blocking a lot of the wind. He tried to find what little string or rope he had to tie the coats down. The problem was that he was having difficult seeing where things were in the blinding snow. The way the snow was blowing, it was a total white-out.

IDIOT ALERT! IDIOT ALERT! IDIOT ALERT!

A sudden realization hit him. A complete white-out. He could barely see the lower branches of the tree that he was hiding under. He could not see any of the trees that were close by. If he could not see trees that were less than four feet away from him, the guards in the towers should not be able to see anything at all past their noses.

He crawled out from under the blanketing coats and then out from under the tree. It was a full blowing blizzard and the perfect opportunity to get out of here. He checked the compass – which now had become even more precious in his life. All he had to do was keep it close to his face, pray that the blizzard kept on going for a while and use all of the supplies that he had been utilizing for his escape plan.

He took all of the equipment and bundled Marie up with and in it. She kept on looking at him. She somehow seemed to be showing some emotion now. Her normal stare had been totally void of any emotion or clue as to what she was thinking. She had been able to respond, in a lucid manner, to all of his questions, so he knew her brain was working, he just could not tell what her attitude was. He was a little baffled at the difference but did not have the time to contemplate or investigate it. No matter, once they were across, he hoped he would get an explanation on everything.

She was disgusted. Now he was telling her that he was planning on executing some bone-brained plan to crawl across the minefield, get to the fence and what...just do a little hop over it? How was he supposed to pull that one off? She had been trying to act indifferent to anything he said, but now...he really irked her. He was going to crawl to the fence...right under the noses of all of the guards and dog patrols, set up some kind of wool and rubber bridge over the fence and they would be home free. He was now seeming to be even dumber than what she had first thought of him. Good choice for a patsy, except for a screwed up imagination...and the fact that her original plan had gone totally awry.

This part of the trip was going to be very different. Before he had been walking while pulling the sled. Now, he was going to have to crawl on his stomach. He pulled the sled out from under the tree, checked the compass and started walking. Here among the trees he did not need to hide, especially during a white-out. Even more, with the blizzard he had no reason for hiding at all. Here among the trees he had memorized it during the last eleven days, so moving in here was second nature. He found the really big tree that he had hidden under in order to do his reconnaissance of the guards.

Now, down to his stomach and start pulling. He pulled with his hands and kicked with his feet. After several kicks and pulls he lay there confused. There were two very small trees, just two or three feet ahead of him, from what he remembered. He should have found them by now. He checked the compass – yes, correct heading. He waved his hands ahead of him – nothing. What was wrong? Then he noticed that the snow behind where he had been pulling with his arms was a lot deeper. He realized that he had been swimming in place in the deep snow and just moving the fresh snow to a pile behind him. He growled in frustration.

He reached into the coat and pulled out two bayonets. He used them to stab the ground and pull himself forward. After just three pulls, he found himself between the two small trees. He heaved a sigh of relief.

Stab, pull. Stab, pull. Stab, pull. Stab, pull, Stab, pull. Check the compass. Stab, pull. Stab, pull. Stab, pull. Stab, pull, Stab, pull. Check the compass.

He had no idea how far he had gone, but he figured that he was past the point of no return. If the wind and snow stopped now, he would be caught – or shot. Keep going at all costs. He really had nothing else to lose.

Stab, pull. Stab, pull. Stab, pull. Stab, pull, Stab, pull. Check the compass. The snow under him felt a little different here.

He pushed some of it aside and realized that he was on the asphalt. He pushed himself up to his hands and knees and went as fast as he could across the road. Some idiot just might be brave (or stupid) enough to be driving out here right now. "No point in getting run over by someone who is...doing something equally as stupid and crazy as what I'm doing," he said out loud.

He then felt another twang of stupidity hit him. He had been thinking of doing that belly crawl over the minefield. Spread the weight out by being in the prone position and there would be less chance of setting a mine off. He had no need of crawling until he reached the other side of the road. Then another thought hit him: He had learned that he needed to use the bayonets, in the first few feet of this part of the journey. Okay – lesson learned. No stupidity in that part. Learn a lesson and utilize it.

Once he felt the ground change, again, under his feet, he turned back and made sure that he still had the sled. He then went down to the ground and started the crawl again.

Stab, pull. Stab, pull. Stab, pull. Stab, pull, Stab, pull. Check the compass. He was keeping a good heading. He turned the compass a few times to make sure that it was not affected by the wind or the cold. No problem whatsoever. It is an inanimate object, with a needle that performs one single function.

Stab, pull. Stab, pull. Stab, pull. Stab, pull, Stab, pull. Check the compass. The ice beneath him felt very smooth. He pulled on the shoulder harness every now and again to check and make sure he still had the sled. Once again he marveled at whoever designed the thing as a snow sled did a wonderful job. All of that weight on it and it still moved with minimum effort on snow or ice.

Stab, pull. Stab, pull. Stab, pull. Stab, pull, Stab, pull.
Check the compass. It was getting very tiresome, however, he could
not afford to slow down or stop. A blizzard could last for a few
day, a few hours, or…who knows? He stopped several times as he
was going along. He did not want to spend too much time resting
because, again, he had no idea how long the blizzard would last.

Stab, pull. Stab, pull. Stab, pull. Stab, pull, Stab, pull. Check
the compass. He felt his feet getting a little cold. He wondered
how Marie was getting along. She could not move at all. The only
reason that his upper body and arms were warm was because of
the constant motion. A constant motion that was the result of total
desperation.

Stab, pull. Stab, pull. Stab, pull. Stab, pull, Stab, pull.
Check the compass. He had figured that the open field was at least
100 yards from the road to the fence. He scoffed in disgust. Nice
big killing field for the kind and benevolent guards who are saving
the fun loving communist citizens from the sadistic decadence of the
West.

Stab, pull. Stab, pull. Stab, pull. Stab, pull, Stab, pull.
Check the compass. He figured that by now he was approximately
one fourth of the way across. If it had not been for the compass, he
knew that he would have probably been going…who knows where.

Stab, pull. Stab, pull. Stab, pull. Stab, pull, Stab, pull. His
arms started to get a little tired. Yes, he could walk forever, as Marie
had observed. This was not walking. He wished that he had gone to
the gym for a bit of weight lifting. Some extra upper body strength
would sure come in handy right now.

Stab, pull. Stab, pull. Stab, pull. Stab, pull, Stab, pull.
Maybe a third of the way…maybe. Keep thinking positive. Each
pull got him closer to the fence – closer to freedom and not having
to hide all the time - anymore.

Stab, pull. Stab, pull. Stab, pull. Stab, pull, Stab, pull. He
did not know what was more tiring – the pain in his arms or the
monotony of pulling without being able to see the goal – the fence.
Go for the unknown! The fence will be in sight…sooner or later.
Probably later, but keep going.

Stab, pull. Stab, pull. Stab, pull. Stab, pull, Stab, pull. On
and on he went. He kept on trying to estimate where he was by now.
He realized that each time he tried to think of how much distance
he had covered the pain in his arms seemed to subside a little. Of
course! That is it! The mind can concentrate on only one thing at
a time. Stop thinking about the pain and fatigue in his arms and
concentrate on something else. He tried singing, he tried reciting
some of the poems that had been crammed down his throat in school
and he tried thinking of anything to keep his mind off his arms. He
did, however, not forget to occasionally check the compass.

Stab, pull. Stab, pull. Stab, pull. Stab, pull, Stab, pull. He
was suddenly having a hard time breathing. Something seemed to
be blocking his nose. He realized that the ice was building up on
his mustache. He used one of the bayonets to shave the ice away. It
pulled a few hairs out as well but that was the least of his problems
right now.

Stab, pull. Stab, pull. Stab, pull. Stab, pull, Stab, pull. All
of a sudden the ground seemed to slope down a little. He wondered
why it dropped down. Then he remembered - the dog patrols near

the fence. This would be packed down a lot more and thus lower than the rest of the area. Was he finally within spitting distance of the fence? He started inching forward. The fence was close by and was electrified. He did not want to find the fence with the bayonets. Forward, inch by inch, while straining his eyes.

There it is! Between torrents of flying snow, he saw it less than two feet away. Finally something other than white was in front of his eyes. He laughed like a drunken idiot for a few moments. He had made it across the minefield by skimming across ice that was, in all probability, at least eight inched thick.

Then he got back to the serious task at hand. He went back to Marie and pulled the snow shield away from her face. "We are at the fence," he shouted triumphantly. Now he saw shock in her eyes. She did not blink. All that time he was pulling her and there was nothing but a deadpan stare. Now, was she acting or showing…emotions? Had she suddenly started healing? No time for philosophy or medical cogitations. He had to get to work.

She stared at him in shock and disbelief. She knew that she had been pulled along. Pulled at a much slower rate than what he had normally been doing. For her to believe that they were right there at the fence was just too big a whopper of a lie for her to swallow. Maybe he was just trying to humor her…before…what? She was not buying any part of his…tall tale. Bonehead Bradley was just making up another one of his stories…because… (?). How could someone as incompetent as he, get her, in her helpless condition, this far and now, possibly to the other side of the fence with one of the most asinine plans that she had ever heard of?

Now was the time to put the plan into motion. He pulled

two coats out. He laid one of them on his side of the fence. It immediately was snagged on the barbs on the wire. The other one was draped over the other side. Put the collars and arms at the top of the fence, with the rest of it draped down to the ground. The barbed wire kept them in place.

He was extremely grateful that the fence was just over four feet high. He had heard that there were parts of it that were over ten feet high, with razor wire on top. Apparently they had not gotten to this part of the fence with the tall stuff. It must have cost a fortune for all that fencing. According to the communists, it was worth the expenditure to keep the Soviet citizens safe from the west.

He started laying the rubber sheets over the coats. Problem: The wind was blowing the rubber all about. They were not getting snagged on the barbed wire because they were not touching the barbs – only the coats. He had to take any string that he had left, poke holes in the ends of the rubber sheets, lace them together and then tie them to the coats. This was mildly successful. It was also an irritatingly long and slow process.

Three times he felt as if the wind was subsiding and nearly panicked. If it slowed enough – he would be seen and the escapade would be over. He could not stop or even slow down, because there might never be another chance at this. This was absolutely the point of no return. Do it now...or die...or be recaptured by the Russians and face...enormous consequences.

He finally got the rubber blanket over the coat on the east side. He was having a tough time trying to figure out how to tie the west side down. Forget it! That would mean pulling the coat back (off of the barbs) and lacing it on this side and then throw it back over. He picked Marie up off of the sled and stood her up. "I'm going to drop you over to the other side of the fence," he shouted.

Her eyes were wide open now. She was definitely showing an emotion. Why did she wait until now?

"Do you understand? I am going to drop you over onto the west side of the fence...into West Germany."

One blink, followed by a reaction that left no question as to what she was experiencing – astonishment.

He heaved a sigh of relief. He then picked her up and put her feet over the fence. He then pushed the upper part of her body away from the fence, in an attempt at keeping her from contacting any part of the electrified death. She fell into the snow with a sound like: Fwump! He could not see where she landed but he had not heard (or smelled) any sizzling.

Next was the sled. Without her on the thing it almost seemed weightless. He tossed it to the right, over the fence, away from where he had pushed her. Anything else that he had been dragging with him, he now threw it over the fence in the same area as the sled. He now took the lacing that was attached to the bottom of the rubber blanket and the coat and stuck it in his teeth. He crawled over the fence. Once his body was over, he pushed himself away before he could touch any exposed fence. He stood there a moment with his heart pounding...and started giggling again. He pulled the laces out of his mouth and peeled the covers on the east side of the fence over to the west side. He felt that it would be even more frustrating to the Russians if they did not know how or where he had escaped... or even the fact that he had escaped. Leaving any evidence would or could give them a reason to try for some kind of extradition. He was not sure what the laws were, however, there was probably some manipulative politician, somewhere, who would try.

The wind was still blowing hard so he did have enough time to pull his entire bridge off of the fence. He peeled the coat off of the west side and started looking for Marie and all of the equipment. Most of it was buried in about a foot of soft powdery snow. It took quite a while to find her, all of the equipment and the sled.

Initially he could not find her - until he tripped over her. He found her face. Her eyes were clenched shut and he could see that her lips were turning blue. He quickly used the coats and rubber sheets that he had used to shield the fence to cover her and bundle her up.

He could not do much else for her until he had some way of getting out of sight of the fence – even from this side. One of the initial briefings said: "Once a person is on the west side, the Russian guards are not allowed to shoot anymore. If they do then the people on the west side are allowed to return fire." Of course that applied to the checkpoints in Berlin. In Berlin, there were American guards on the west side of the checkpoints. He had no idea where he was, but he knew that there was no way that he was anywhere near Berlin. He was also sure that he was not close to any check or crossing point.

After finding all of the gear and getting her even more bundled up with most of it, he checked his compass and headed west – again. On this side of the fence, there was no need for a clear killing field. The trees and brush were rather dense. He quickly found another large evergreen and decided that this would be as good a place as any, to get out of the wind. He had not taken more than twenty paces away from the fence, however, that did not matter at all…now. They were on the west side of the fence. They were in WEST Germany. They were now safe from the Russian guards.

He crawled under the low branches, pulled the sled in behind him and started getting the coats and rubber ready to wrap around and share warmth. He had all the warmth. She was shivering. She could not do very much of anything, but she could feel the cold. As he was trying to huddle closer, he discovered that she had wet herself again. He growled to himself in frustration. He changed the diaper as quickly as possible and then snuggled as close as he could. It seemed to take forever before she finally stopped shivering. He felt for a pulse to make sure she was still alive - and then felt rather stupid. If she was shivering, of course she was still alive. Dead people don't shiver. He had found the pulse and then let sleep take over to cure his exhaustion.

For quite some time she stared at him. She was beyond flabbergasted. The bone-brained bungling butthead from the backward burg of bunghole Georgia had done it. He had beaten all the odds against the Russian winter. He had crossed the frontier on foot, dragging a helpless invalid with him. He had survived on raw meat almost the entire way. After having crossed from Russia through either Poland or Czechoslovakia or East Germany, he had used the weather to aid him in escaping from behind the iron curtain. They were in West Germany and he had achieved it by the most idiotic plan that she had ever heard in her life. It was so idiotic – that it had worked.

Then she started getting doubts again. Had he done all of

that...posturing, just to make her think that they were on the other side? That would be an awful lot of trouble...just to have to admit... in the morning...that it was a ruse. If this was some kind of a trick, he would have some mammoth kind of explaining to do if...NO, what kind of an imbecile would possibly do that? She pondered for several moments. Someone who was stupid enough to fall for her little scheme of looking for a mythical enemy agent. The morning was going to be very interesting. If he was telling the truth, he had pulled off something that would embarrass the life out of the KGB and something that he could not tell anyone about. It would fascinate everyone in the CIA and would make interesting reading for every field agent...for the rest of time that the CIA and the USA existed.

She sighed. 'What a mess!'

She decided that all of her speculation would amount to nothing. In the morning he would do...heaven alone knows what. Wait until then to find out. For now, stop shivering, accept his body warmth and sleep.

She tried to growl at herself. How do you sleep when you are not tired? She had been laying on this confounded sled for... weeks? Months? How long? Now that he claimed that they were on the other side of the fence, she just could not sleep form the excitement (and bewilderment) of how all of this had happened.

She would just have to wait until morning and/or when the blizzard was over and then listen to anything and everything around her to find out if he was telling the truth. For now all she could do was lay there and feel hungry and confused.

17

He had no clue how long he had slept. He knew that he was stiff and hungry…and wet. She had done it again. He crawled out from under the covers and started the morning ritual of cleaning her and getting food…oh! Food? In his haste he had left all of the snares behind – in place. All of the "food" was approximately 180 yards "east" of their current location, on the other side of that horrid fence. Breakfast, this morning, would consist entirely of snow. He did not have enough string left that would make a decent snare. He also had zero bait. Who cares, it is snow on the *west* side of the fence. If there were any rabbits caught in the snares, they would hang there, die and freeze to death, until the thaw…and then rot. Too bad.

Marie lay there staring at him the entire time. He had wondered about a few things when the trek had been going on, but it seemed trivial at the time. Now, he had a little time to find out a few things. He sighed and prepared for the questioning.

"I want to ask you a few questions."

One blink. 'You've got questions? Just wait until I can talk…then I've got a few questions of my own, buster!'

"When I first met you, you said that you were an Airman First Class – is that your true rank?"

Two blinks. 'How much should I give him? Let's play him and see what he's looking for.'

"Are you enlisted?"

Two blinks. 'Make him think I outrank him...why not?'

"Officer?"

One blink. 'Of course, dummy. If I'm not enlisted, I have to be an officer.'

"Butter Bar?" he inquired.

Two blinks. 'Oh PLEASE! No way.'

"First Looey?"

Two blinks. 'That's ridiculous as well.'

He sighed. "Captain?" He wondered how far up the ladder he was going to have to go.

She did not react immediately to this one. She looked as if she were deep in thought. Then – one blink. 'Why not? I don't want to be too crazy with him. If I told him that I was a Major, that could tie me to that phony investigation at CBPO...if any of this information ever got back to that base.'

"Is Marie...Wilkins, or Williams or Walker or whatever you said, your real name?"

Two blinks. 'Wilkins? Williams? Where is your mind? Dummy!'

"Right now, I'm going to go with Captain Marie...which was it? Was it Wilkins?"

Two blinks. 'Think dummy.' She mentally projected "Walker" to him.

"Williams?"

Two blinks. She mentally scoffed. 'NOT IMPORTANT!'

"Walker?"

One blink. 'You win a kewpie doll...dummy.'

He sighed. "Okay, Captain Marie Walker, let's see if we can find you a hospital."

One blink. 'Yeah, it would be nice to find one...if we are *really* on the west side of the fence.' She was still in disbelief at what had happened. Now, for the first time since the crash, she actually had hope for survival. Whatever had happened to her, she desperately hoped that some surgeon could reverse the damage and make her whole again. If not...her only desire was to die.

After doing what he could with wet clothing, rubber sheets, equipment, bundling up Marie on the sled and smiling while he realized the he did not need to worry about security measures anymore, he put the harness on his shoulders and started walking again. This time...he did not have to worry about cover, though. This time the open area would be great. All the time he had been on the other side of the fence, he had done everything he could to avoid people, open areas and roads. Now these were precisely what he was looking for. Any open area, any person, and any road... whatever. Find something or someone and get out of this nightmare completely.

He thought about it as he was walking through the brush. What little German he knew, just might not help very much. Mainly, he knew just enough of the German language to either get a prostitute in bed or – if she was not a "lady of the evening" – get his face slapped. He could not think of much more to say that would be helpful. He grunted in disgust. Marie knows German, fluently. Now would be a good time for her to open up her big fat mouth and start yapping – in German.

He walked on. He had to go through some of the thickest brush he had gone through during the entire ordeal. It did not really matter. Now, he did not have to worry about being quiet. He did not have to worry about what might be beyond that next tree. The burden was a lot lighter now that he was in the west.

He came to a clearing and looked around. Hallelujah, it was a road! It had been covered over during the blizzard, however, there were a few of the markers that you always see alongside the roads everywhere. So – which way? North or south? It did not make any difference now. For some reason he could not make up his mind. If he went north, he would be headed for Denmark. If he headed south, he would be headed for Austria. Who cares, he was in Western Europe and he did not have to worry about any Russians chasing after him…here.

Just as he decided to head south, he heard a vehicle approaching – from the north. He wondered what kind of an idiot would be driving in this mess, right after a blizzard. Then he remembered a big snow storm back in South Carolina at Shaw AFB. The first things on the roads were the snow plows. It had to be the same thing here. Nothing else made any sense. The best thing to do was hope that they, whoever they are, can speak English. Otherwise things could get really difficult.

The vehicle came around a corner into his view. He nearly

laughed out loud. It was a US Army halftrack, and it was plowing its own path down the snow covered road. It was having very little trouble moving snow off to the side as it slowly moved south. There were two men in the cab and they were smoking cigarettes. Tobacco! Something that he had not smelled in quite some time. He did not smoke, however, the smell was one that would be from civilization...even though it stinks.

He stepped out onto the road and started waving at the driver. He could see the two men in the cab looking at him with shock on their faces. The truck slowed a little as it approached. He stepped to the side and sighed with relief.

The truck stopped. The driver rolled his window down and he looked at Bradley rather confused. *"Nicht verstehen Deutsche,"* he said quickly.

"I don't speak too much of that lingo, myself," said Bradley with his best Georgia twang.

The driver was momentarily taken aback by hearing English, especially with a pronounced accent. He looked at his partner and then back at Bradley. He opened his mouth as if to say something and then looked as if he were having trouble trying to figure out what to say. "Uh...who are...you and what're you doing in this area?" He looked back at his partner again as if looking for some kind of reassurance.

Bradley hung his head. He looked up and said: "Look, I don't have time for a long story right now. I need for you to take me..." He pointed at the sled. "...and my colleague to the nearest US Military Base...to a hospital."

The driver laughed. "Your colleague is a sled? Buddy, you been out playing in the snow too long. You got a brain freeze and it's makin' your thoughts crazy."

"There's a woman on that sled and she's hurt," growled Bradley. "She needs to be in a hospital, NOW! I don't have time to explain what's going on or what's happened. She needs medical attention – now!"

"Right!" The driver scoffed at him. "Look, if you are US Military personnel, you should know that you shouldn't be inside the ten klick zone. You're in the zone. Matter of fact, this part of the road is less than one kilometer from the fence, so you're in violation of all kinds of regulations for being here."

Bradley clenched his teeth. "You're not supposed to be inside the ten klick zone – UNLESS YOU HAVE AUTHORIZATION! We are authorized to be here, because of what we were doing." He tried to hold his temper, however this jerk was making things very difficult.

The driver mocked him. "Authorization? What authorization do you have?"

Bradley's brain slammed to a halt. What could he say? Oh, yes! When all else fails: "What's your security clearance?"

The driver had a stupid look on his face. He looked back at his partner then back to Bradley. "What's that got to do with it?"

"If your security clearance isn't high enough, I can't tell you what I'm doing here…other than the fact that we're on official business. Even if you're clearance is high enough, you still have to have the 'need to know' before I could tell you anything."

The driver looked a little irritated. "Secret!" he spat.

"Not good enough," said Bradley. "I can't tell you what's going on. All I can tell you is that my partner and is hurt, and we need transportation...to a hospital."

The driver gave Bradley a smug smile. "If'n you can't tell me what or why, then I can't give you and the other one a ride. Main reason I won't give you a ride is because I don't want to have to go back and do all the paperwork on someone I picked up, inside the ten klick zone. It takes too much time and I don't like having to do it...for anybody." With that the halftrack lurched forward.

Bradley could hear both of them laughing even over that noise being made by the halftrack.

Marie was laying there getting madder and madder as the conversation continued. 'Just pull out one of the rifles and pretend that yo-yo is a rabid fox,' she thought facetiously.

He quickly went to the sled, pulled a rifle out of the rubber holster he had made for it, brought it up to his shoulder, aimed and fired.

Marie gasped in shock. 'I didn't mean it you dummy!'

The driver side rear-view mirror fragmented as the bullet tore through it. The halftrack stopped immediately. Both men jumped out of the truck and looked back at Bradley totally aghast.

The driver looked up at the remains of the frame then back at Bradley. "What's the matter with you?! I tried to do you a favor by not getting you in trouble for being here! Now you go and do this!

Are you nuts or something?"

Marie was confused. 'What'd you shoot?'

Bradley aimed the rifle at the driver. "I don't have time to argue! Now…I am *telling* you – right now – get your butts back here and get the Captain on your truck! You will then take us to the nearest base so that she can get the medical attention she desperately needs! Is there any part of that you don't understand?"

The passenger growled at Bradley: "Boy, you are gonna have a ton of explaining to do, when we get back to the base."

"Fine!" said Bradley. "Just get us there…sometime before the next Presidential election."

"Nixon just took the oath," said the passenger.

Marie mentally scoffed. 'Not the point, you stupid grunt.'

The two men glared at Bradley as the sled was picked up, carried to the truck and lifted up into the rear section. He climbed up inside the truck. Once he was sure that she was as secure as she could be, he sat down next to the sled to make sure that it did not rattle her around.

"You'll be in a hospital soon. Hopefully, they can figure out something to do to help you recover."

'You hope,' she thought. 'What d'you think my feelings on the matter are?'

He was not sure what he was reading in her eyes. Fear? Amazement? Frustration? Respect? Some kind of acknowledgement? Since they had been on the trail, she had shown virtually no emotions of any type. Now, she stared at him with some kind of wonder in her eyes.

She listened to his assurances. She had just found out something else about him – he was very proficient with a rifle – even though it was a Russian rifle. He still knew what to do with it. She was not sure what he had hit, however, it got the attention of the two grunts in the truck and ended a moronic argument. If she had been able, she would have kicked both of those Army numbskulls into unconsciousness and left them in the snow, while she took the truck. This was just as good because at least those two morons knew this area and knew where they were going. She now had the proof that she needed...the two US Army guys...she WAS on the west side of the fence. The Patsy had pulled it off.

The truck lumbered on through heavy snowdrifts for some time. Bradley felt a little motion sickness from it. He had not been a passenger in a vehicle since...the crash. He had no idea how long ago that was.

When he felt the truck stop and he heard voices outside of the vehicle he felt a little more relief. The tailgate of the truck was opened and Bradley was staring down the barrels of three rifles. There was a Lieutenant standing behind the three riflemen, pointing a pistol in the air, looking around in the truck, trying to assess the situation.

Bradley shook his head. 'There's the big and bold Lieutenant, standing behind the riflemen, trying to look like he's in charge. If you're so big and brave, why are you in the rear?' he thought.

"Don't make any sudden movements," barked the Lieutenant.

"These men told me of the stunt you pulled on the perimeter road. I'm not going to put up with any more stupidity."

Bradley started laughing. "Then, Sir, why are you putting up with those two…sorry excuses for grunts?"

"They're doing their duty," snapped the Lieutenant.

"They were trying to shirk their duty on the perimeter road, Sir," said Bradley through his giggling. "They told me to go west about nine klicks and that they'd pick the two of us up there. They didn't want to have to do the paperwork, of finding military personnel inside the ten klick zone."

"He's fibbin', Sir," whined the driver.

Bradley laughed even harder. "The Captain here is *hurt*! She's not dead or *deaf*. She heard what you two idiots said. Once the doctors have had a good look at her and they get her back to where she can talk, then, I'll be happy to listen to *her* story." He leaned forward. "Will *you*?"

The driver flushed. He looked at the Lieutenant and made a few unintelligible noises. He then put his hands over his face and groaned.

The passenger was observing a tree off to his left, with a very red face.

The Lieutenant looked at the driver trying to read his face and actions. He looked up at Bradley with a little disgust on his face. "Come out slowly, no tricks."

Bradley ease his way out of the halftrack. 'It'd be just my luck,' he thought. 'All that time in the communist countryside, facing hungry wolves and a rabid fox…survive all of that and then get shot by some trigger-happy grunt.' He saw a military ambulance with medical personnel standing by as he stepped out of the vehicle. He was immediately pushed up against the halftrack and frisked. The found all of the bayonets and all of the other junk that he had carried around in his pockets during the trip. He chuckled as the Lieutenant frowned while looking at that precious little compass. That highly valuable piece of equipment that had led him all the way to the border. He gave them no resistance as they cuffed him and led him to a jeep.

"Hold on there!" someone shouted.

Everyone looked in the direction of the man that hollered. It was one of the medical personnel from the ambulance. He was hurrying towards them.

"I need to talk to that man for a few minutes," he said.

"Excuse me," said the Lieutenant. "This man is being taken away for questioning about…"

"I don't care about that," said the man. "I've looked at the woman and she is totally helpless. She can't respond to anything. I need to find out as much as I can from him."

"Sir, I'm the one in charge of this prisoner and I…"

"And I'm a Major… Lieutenant! I require something about what happened to her otherwise I'm going to be playing a very long guessing game." He looked at Bradley. "Can I trust you to tell me what happened to her?"

Bradley smiled at the doctor. "Not a problem at all, Sir."

"All right, start at the beginning…when the injury happened."

"Yes, Sir. We were in a vehicle…and it got hit by a landslide of some sort."

The Lieutenant scoffed. "Some sort? What's that supposed to mean?"

The Major clenched his teeth. "Lieutenant…please…you weren't there so shut up."

Bradley gave the Lieutenant a rather dirty look. "I don't know whether it was an avalanche or a rock slide. All I know is that one second we were driving along, then BAM…we're being shoved over a cliff." He turned back to the Major. "I don't know how far we tumbled down that hill, but…there was all kinds of debris inside the vehicle that was flying around while we were tumbling. When we came to a sudden stop, I saw a great big bruise on her forehead. Before the crash – she was totally functioning. After the crash… she's been like that. She can't speak, she can barely move…I had to cut all of her food into very tiny pieces or else she couldn't eat because she can't open her mouth very wide. She can only respond to yes/no questions with eye blinks."

The Major nodded. "How long ago did this happen?"

Bradley hung his head. "Sir…I completely lost track of time. When this…mess began, I was clean shaven. Look at my beard. That's how long ago the accident happened."

The Major looked closely at the beard in shock. He closed his eyes and grunted. He sighed. He smiled at Bradley. "Did you notice any other injuries on her…immediately after the accident?"

"No, Sir. She was just...incapable of...doing anything for herself. Nothing!"

The Major sighed again. "Okay, thank you." He looked at the Lieutenant. "Now, you can take him away."

They took him to a lockup where the Lieutenant took the two men from the halftrack off somewhere else to talk to them.

Bradley smiled as he entered the jail cell. He saw a bed. Four beds actually. There were two sets of bunk beds in the cell. He dropped his coat, went to one of the beds, flopped down...on a BED! With a PILLOW! And a BLANKET! And clean SHEETS! He chuckled as he fondled the wool military blanket. "At least the thing is not gray. It is olive drab." After that thought, he was asleep almost immediately.

He was awakened for lunch. He relished what was on the plate. It was meatloaf, mashed potatoes and corn...and it was WARM. It actually had a pleasant smell. It was not cold, raw rabbit. There was one of those little cardboard containers of milk. Usually he had hated to drink milk. Now, compared to all of the melted snow he had had to endure, it was better than any French Champagne. It was heavenly. He chewed slowly on each mouthful of food. He drank the milk slowly. He had never savored any meal like he did this one before...especially the milk.

After finishing his feast, he was taken to an interrogation room and asked a few questions about his identity. He only told them: Name, rank, service number, the unit he was assigned to at Rhein Main, his commanding officer and that he was not sure whether they had the need to know what he had been doing.

He was then taken to a place to take a shower. Once again he was in heaven. While in the shower, his clothing was cleaned. Again – heaven.

When he went back to the cell, he had to sleep on a different bed. The one he had use stunk to high heaven. He shook his head. 'A few hours ago…that was me,' he thought.

18

Bradley was taken out of his cell to a different drab looking room where there was only one table, two chairs and a big mirror. He was told to sit in the chair that faced the mirror. He had a pretty good idea of what this was and what was going to happen.

A Major walked into the room. Bradley stood up at attention. The Major walked over to the other chair slowly. He sat down and looked Bradly up and down.

"Sit down…Sergeant Dooley…if…that is your name," said the Major flatly.

Bradley sat down. "That is my name and rank, Sir."

"Well, I am Major Delgado and I am going to be talking to you about your situation. I have contacted your Commanding Officer and he confirms that there is a Sergeant Bradley F. Dooley assigned there. This Sergeant, however, happens to be assigned temporarily…somewhere else. They have a set of orders there but they don't know where you are or how long he is supposed to be gone."

"Yes, Sir, that's what they were told."

"So…who is Captain Walker? Why won't you tell me anything about what you…and the Captain were doing?"

Bradley sighed and hung his head. He looked up. "Sir, I am a Sergeant. She is a Captain. She was in charge. If you're going to get any information about our doings, comings and goings, you're going to have to get it from her. I really am not sure exactly what we were doing…or why. She kept me in the dark as well. She just needed me for…reasons that I don't understand myself…yet."

Delgado shook his head. "You're telling me that you've been cavorting around with that Captain for three and a half months and you can't tell me anything of what the two of you were doing and where you went? How do you expect me to believe that?"

"Sir, she told me…THREE AND A HALF MONTHS?" Bradley sat there stunned. "It was…that long?"

Delgado simply nodded.

Bradley took several deep breaths. He shook his head and sniffed. "Sir…she told me one thing, then something else happened. She said that we were going to go one place and then I got surprised at the last second. What we were doing…I can only guess. Even if I did know…exactly what we were doing – I still don't think that I could discuss it with you…without permission from the proper authority."

Delgado smiled. "Well…who is this…proper authority? I mean this Captain Walker has to have a Commanding Officer as well. Who is that?"

Bradley searched his memory for anything. Then it hit him – the marriage certificate. "Major, the only name that I know of, other than the Captain I worked with, is a man named Samuel Bates. I don't know his rank…other than that he is an officer, or even his branch of service. I don't know where he's stationed. The only paperwork that Captain Walker showed me, with a name on it, was that one piece that had the name...Samuel Bates." He sat up in surprise. "Wait a minute! The orders! Someone had to sign those orders! Get with my CO and get that copy of the orders! That might give you something." He hoped that would suffice for now. He had no other names to go on.

Delgado had a skeptical look. "That's all that you're going to give me?"

"That's all that I have, Major," he said desperately. "I really don't know that I have any permission to tell you or anyone else about what happened. I don't know if you have the need to know. Even if I did tell you...I doubt that you'd believe me...without confirmation from Captain Walker."

"So that's it."

"That's all...unless you can tell me what happened to Captain Walker."

Delgado stared at Bradley with a blank expression. "You don't have the need to know."

Bradley sat there poker faced. 'Typical smart-alec, manipulative, childish answer that an officer would give. Manipulate your words and use them against you.'

Delgado stood up. Bradley snapped to attention. Delgado left the room. Bradley sat down.

A few moments later the door opened up again. Bradley was a little surprised to see an Army Military Policeman and an Air Force Air Policeman walk in together.

The MP did all the talking. "We're not sure what to do with

you right now. All I know is that we're supposed to keep an eye on you."

The AP pulled handcuffs off his belt. Bradley gave no resistance as he was cuffed and led away again. These two men took him to a waiting M35 truck. He was a little surprised that his limousine was going to be a two and a half ton truck, however at this point he was in no mood to argue. Just let it happen and wait to see exactly what does happen. They put him in the back of the big truck and threw the canvas flap down. He had no idea where he was being taken.

The drive took a lot longer than what he had expected. Maybe they were playing another head game with him. Marie had certainly done that. Why should they be different?

Screw it! Lay down and take a nap.

The truck finally stopped. The flap was opened up. He was told to get out of the truck. He got up and tried to blink the sleep out of his eyes.

While the AP checked the cuffs, Bradley got a little curious. "Hey, guys, can you tell me where I am?"

The AP looked at him and blankly stated: "Hof Air Base, Republic of West Germany."

Bradley looked to his left, then his right, then up, then down. "Hey, guys, can you tell me where I am?"

The AP snickered. "I guess that you've never heard of Hof Air Base."

"You guess right, I haven't. I don't have a clue where I am."

"Hof AB – about 20 kilometers from East Germany and not much farther to Czechoslovakia. Poland isn't that far away either. Nice little corner of West Germany to be sitting in. We could get hit from both the north and the east. They could be on us before we know it. I just pray that they don't try."

They took him to a barber. He was a little surprised that it had taken this long. They cuffed him to the chair.

The barber looked at the AP. "So? What do I do with him?"

"You get him back into compliance with Air Force regulations. He claims to be Air Force and has been in the field… for some time. Apparently without any shaving equipment."

The barber shrugged, pulled out his clippers and went to work. He gave Bradley a very close haircut and then gave him a clean shave.

"I could have done the shaving," said Bradley, a little disgusted.

The MP spoke up. "We're not allowed to let you get close to something that sharp. They said that you just might be stupid enough to commit suicide."

Bradley grunted. "Who was stupid enough to make that silly accusation – an officer?"

Both of his guards laughed at that comment.

Next, they took him to another shower. Just like his last shower, he took his sweet time cleaning himself in water that was as hot as he could stand it. As he scrubbed himself, he felt as if he were still removing numerous layers of crud…one at a time. For the first time since he had entered Russia, he felt clean.

Once he had finished drying himself off, he received a very baggy set of fatigues that had no insignias on the shirt. There were signs that the shirt had belonged to someone else, but he did not care. He was clean shaved, he had been allowed to clean all of the hair off of himself and now he was wearing clothing that was clean…and not Russian.

He was taken to a cell that was much larger than the other one he had been in. The old cell had been set up for four people with two bunk beds and one toilet. His one had only one cot. They could have fit at least six of those bunk beds in this cell. There was a toilet and a sink in this cell. Three of the walls of the cell were nothing but bars. The back wall, with the toilet and sink was cinderblock – *gray* cinderblock. He was really beginning to hate that color. He went in, sat down on the bed and looked around. He laid down on a bed and let out a long sigh of contentment.

19

Bates was sitting at his desk. He was rubbing his hands along the edge, wondering how long it would be before he would no longer have a desk. He and his Aide would end up in jail...or *if* he would end up in jail...somewhere for the stupid act of grabbing that Air Force Sergeant – without any authorization. He wondered what the penalty would be for violating that act.

A courier walked in with an envelope. Bates closed his eyes in contemplation of the worst possible scenario. Some Russian had found that Sergeant Dooley and now it was time for Bates to face the music. He showed his credentials to the courier and took the envelope.

He sighed as he stared at the harmless looking manila envelope. 'No point putting it off,' he thought. 'Just open the rotten thing and find out...now...just how bad it's going to be.' He closed his eyes as he tore the envelope open. He felt one piece of paper inside the envelope. He shook his head. 'One lousy piece of paper that determines the rest of my life.' He pulled it out and unfolded it. Now, he opened his eyes. He read the information...and nearly lost control of his bodily functions. At first he had started reading with his jaws clenched. Now, he sat there with his mouth wide open, rereading the letter...several times.

After realizing that he had just drooled on himself...from sitting there dumbfounded with his mouth wide open, he wiped his mouth and called Burke to come into the office.

Burke walked in with a great deal of trepidation on his face. "I saw the courier and…I'm wondering…if that's the notice of… our…end of career…or eradication…or execution."

Bates shook his head. "I…we…we're okay! We're safe… from…" He looked down at the paper. "By some act of…dumb luck…" He looked back up. "I'm being notified that there's a man claiming to be Sergeant Bradley F. Dooley…currently in the lockup at Hof Air Base…on THIS SIDE of the iron curtain…who says that I'm the only contact that he knows of…as to what he has been doing and where…over the last few months. It also says that he was with a Captain Marie Walker…who is currently in the Regional Medical Center…in Frankfurt…Germany. She's undergoing…" He looked back down at the paper and frowned. "…brain surgery." He looked up. "I wonder if…she was hurt…or are they looking to see if she has one."

Burke was now the one standing there dumbfounded. "He's on this side of the fence? Wait, uh…BOTH of them?"

Bates looked down at the letter. "Both of them…are back here in…West Germany."

Burke smiled, however he still had a look of concern. "So… are we…safe?"

"I don't know…yet." He re-read the letter, shaking his head. "It doesn't say that we're in trouble…" He looked up at Burke with concern on his face as well. "…yet."

"So are you going to go get our Sergeant Dooley and…find out what happened?"

"First...I'm going to the Medical Center and check on this... Captain Marie Walker. I don't know if she's Wintergreen. If she is...when I find Dooley..." He dropped his hands down to his lap and shook his head again. "I can hardly wait to see the report on this one."

"You and me both," said Burke wiping some sweat from his forehead.

Bates got up and headed out of the office. "Is my car gassed up?"

"Yes, Sir, your chariot is ready and awiateth you."

Bates went to his home first. He changed into his Air Force uniform. He looked at himself in the mirror and contemplated. He put a cross on his uniform. He decided that he would visit this... Captain Marie Walker...as a military Chaplain. She is in the hospital and no doctor, or nurse, would ever say no to a visit from a Chaplain.

20

She was rudely awakened by two men who were jostling her, trying to make her wake up, whether she wanted to wake up or not. Both were telling her to wake up.

She looked up at the two men through a haze and saw they were dressed in hospital scrubs. That brought back the realization that she was in a hospital. She lifted her right arm to push them away and...froze in shock. She had lifted her right arm. It felt like it weighed a ton, however, for the first time since the crash, she could mover her arm...more than a quarter of an inch. She lifted the other arm. Again it felt like she was lifting a ton of bricks, but she *could* move both arms. She tested her legs. Both legs were heavy but working. She moved her head back and forth and tried to lift it up. Lifting her head was another massive effort. She realized that many of her muscles had become severely weakened because of the inability that she had suffered from the crash.

The two men continued to jostle her.

"I'm awake," she croaked. Again she froze in shock. She was able to speak...now. She was not sure what had happened, however, if she had had the strength, she would be jumping for joy and running, at full speed, through the halls of... (!) 'Where am I?' She looked at the man on her right. "Where am I?" It hurt to talk, however, it still felt good to be able to communicate with something other than yes/no blinking.

He smiled. "Ma'am, you're at the Frankfurt Regional Medical Center. You're in surgical recovery right now...after having gone through about eight hours of brain surgery. According to what I've got here, the neurosurgeon just did something inside your head to remove a clot that was preventing the synapsis of your brain from getting messages to the rest of your body. He said that the involuntary muscles were working fine, but the voluntary ones were extremely restricted because of where the clot was located in the brain."

"So...I'm okay, now?"

"No Ma'am, not yet. It's gonna be a few weeks...if not months of rehabilitation before everything is back to...okay."

She smiled. "I wanna be back to normal as soon as possible. Bring on the rehab!"

The man shook his head. "No, not yet, Ma'am."

"Why not?"

"Before you get started on the rehabilitation, you're going to have to talk to the Obstetrician."

She frowned. "About what?"

The two men looked at each other confused. "Uh...the baby...Ma'am."

She let out a squawk. "Huh? What baby?"

"Your baby, Ma'am. According to what is in these records of yours...from the initial examination...you are either late second trimester or early third trimester."

Now she made the major effort of lifting her head up. For the first time, she was able to see her swollen abdomen. She flopped her head back down on the pillow and moaned in disbelief. "When did this happen?"

"Uh...Ma'am, if *you* don't know...*I* can't help you."

She closed her eyes. "How soon can I see this...OB/GYN?"

"We can call from here in recovery and...the OB will be waiting in your room when we get there, Ma'am."

She sniffed. "Thank you," she said helplessly.

One of the men went to a phone and the other started pushing the gurney out of the recovery room. She ran several things through her head as she took the journey to the room. She discovered that there was a very large amount of wrappings around her head and was told by her "chauffer" that they had shaved her head in order to perform the surgery. The missing hair was, by far, the least of her worries. She was on the west side of the border and she was getting some badly needed medical attention...and she could see that she was well on her way to a full recovery...with a baby.

She was wheeled into a hospital room where they had a very strange looking bed for her. It took four people, several minutes, to get her on this other bed, because of her weakened condition. She found out that because of her advanced pregnancy, the bed sores and the diaper rash, she would be on this very strange bed, mostly laying on her stomach or side until the sores healed.

The Obstetrician finally walked in as Marie lay there panting from the ordeal of moving.

"Good afternoon, Captain Walker. I'm Major Louise Kelly."

Marie gave her a weak smile. "Are you the…brain surgeon or the OB?"

Louise snickered. "I'm the OB. After all of those hours working on your head, the neurosurgeon is currently taking a nap. Now, I need to ask you…if *you* have any idea how far along you are. From my initial examination…I'd guess that you're around 29 weeks, according to the tests…and my best estimate."

Marie sighed. "I didn't even know that I was pregnant… until I finally saw my big fat gut. I've been…incapacitated for…a few months. So you think…I'm at…or just a little past the seven month mark?"

"That sounds about right. From what I've seen of the examination of you and all of the test results."

She grunted. If she was that far along, she knew that it could not be Dooley. It had to have been that oversexed Spaniard…that she had killed. She let out a long sigh. "If you're thinking of trying to contact the father…the only way to get him…is a séance. He had a very unfortunate accident…right after we had sex." She mentally scoffed. 'Accident my foot! It was that seven-iron that I used to split his stupid skull…right after he raped me. He never knew what hit him…from behind.'

"Oh, my dear, I'm so sorry," said Kelly. "I didn't realize that he was…"

"Don't worry about it. We were NOT going to ever see each other again anyway."

"But...I see that you're still wearing your wedding ring."

She chuckled. "Yeah, I haven't taken it in to sell it yet."

Kelly smiled and nodded. "Anyway, while you're rehabilitating, I'm going to be watching your pregnancy, while Doctor Tucker is going to take care of your neurologic recovery."

She sighed. "Okay, thank you." She closed her eyes. An Obstetrician, a Physical Therapist and a brain buster. She knew that she was not going to be lonely...for a long time.

Kelly pulled the blanket back. "Right now, you're going to get a full rub down with some external medications to take care of that rash on your buttocks and the bed sores...that cover your backside." She frowned. "How did all of this happen?"

Marie chuckled. "It's a very long story...and I don't think that you have the proper security clearance to hear it."

Kelly shook her head. "Ah yes, the military and all of its secrets."

Marie nodded. "Right!" She closed her eyes and calmly accepted the, rather cold, salves and/or ointments that they spread all over her backside. She lay there mentally chuckling. Bradley had had his hands all over her and now someone else was doing the same. She was not sure whether or not she approved of all of this fondling, however, this time it *was* for medical reasons.

After the potions had been administered, she was left alone. About an hour later, she heard a familiar voice.

"Excuse me...*Captain*...Walker. It is I...Chaplain Samuel Bates."

She was currently positioned on the bed with her back to the door, in order to give the bed sores a chance to heal. She did not move, she just responded. *"Chaplain…Bates…what a surprise."*

"I'll bet!" He walked around to where she could see him. "I'm confused as to how you…" He looked around suspiciously to see if anyone else was in the room. "…Agent Wintergreen…and plus one…got to this side of the fence. Who assisted you?"

She snorted. "Dumb, stupid luck, a blinding blizzard…and a hard-headed Georgia boy that didn't know when or how to quit… and who can walk forever."

Bates chuckled. "I'm sorry, but you're going to have to elaborate a little bit more on that very rambling and confusing statement."

"I can't…at this time. I went to Moscow with…what'd you call him…plus one?" She chuckled. "I made contact with my people and gave them the instructions. I never was able to get back with them, because we got nabbed. On the way to someplace that they called 'Area 5', we crashed. The truck that we were in went rolling down a hill and…I don't know much after that because… plus one…was pulling me on a sled the rest of the way. He told me stories of his exploits over wolves, rabid foxes and rivers along the way. I don't know what's fact or fiction. You'll have to ask him. Sorry, I wasn't able to complete the mission."

"But you did."

"Huh?"

"It was your contacts that radioed us and told us that the

whole thing was a hoax. The Russians came up with a story that was just too...tempting. We had to send people in to find out and they were waiting...for all of you."

She looked at him in shock. "How many...did we lose?"

"We only lost one. There was another...one of our allies... that lost over forty."

She grimaced. "That stinks!"

"Yeah, but because of your contacts, we let all of the others know...covertly, of course, that it *was* a complete scam."

"Incredible," she chuckled. "I nearly got killed and yet...it was all worth it. Plus I still got back...because of that numbskull that I brought with me."

"Speaking of that...have you ever heard of *Posse Comitatus*?"

She looked at him confused. "Posse...come and what us?"

He cleared his throat. He leaned forward and pronounced it carefully and slowly. "*Posse Comitatus.*"

She looked up nervously. "Can't say that I have. Why? Is it important?"

He sniffed, scratched his nose and smiled. "I'll make sure that you get a copy of it and I'm going to make sure that you read it." He gave her a grim look. "Mandatory reading for YOU!"

"Does it have anything to do with Sergeant Dooley?"

"It has everything to do with him. Speaking of him...should I go get a briefing from him?"

"Of course! He's the one who dragged me...all over the countryside in Russia and...I don't know...maybe Poland...and Czechoslovakia...and maybe East Germany. Whatever he did, you'll have to talk to him to find out."

"Okay, I figured that I would. Is there anything else that you want to tell me at this time?"

She blew a raspberry. "One...I'm approximately seven months pregnant, so after the baby is born...I'm going to have to sit at a desk...for a long time. Two...they've got too much information on me...on the other side, so that was my last field assignment...on the other side of the iron curtain. Three...when we got back to this side...there were a couple of US Army types...that were ready to drive right past us. I'm on that sled...helpless. I heard Dooley tell them that I was hurt and that they should put me on their truck and get me to the hospital. They said that they didn't want to have to do the paperwork...and that he should drag me, on the sled, about nine kilometers due west...*then* they would pick us up. Dooley had to pull out one of those Russian rifles, do a wild west shot and force them to put me on the truck...at gun point. Then, when they got to their Base...they lied to their Commander about what had happened. If Dooley needs a statement from me...about what happened...tell him and those Army people that I concur with Dooley's story. The Army personnel on the truck were absolutely negligent and shirking their duty. It was bad enough that I couldn't move or talk...but for them to tell him that he had to drag me another nine kilometers, just so they didn't have to do any paperwork, before they would assist me...that was just *too* much to take."

Bates nodded. "Good to know." He looked up in thought.

"I'll have some people come in to check on you...now and then. I may think of a few more questions before I head to Hof and get a debriefing from Dooley. Think a little more on anything that you can tell me about your mission. Once you've completed your rehabilitation I'll expect a full report...or at least a little more than what you're telling me now." He turned to get ready to go and stopped. "Wait a moment! How did you get in touch with your contacts...and they got the information to me, but, you didn't find out that...they had contacted us?"

She sighed. "I sent a one word message to my contact. It's a signal. She goes to a subway station in Moscow. In the women's bathroom, in one of the commode stalls, she plants an off-white bra. I go there, like I'm just going to the bathroom. I trade brassieres. In the bra that I leave there, I give them the written instructions or questions. They...apparently contacted you directly. They never did get back with me...and...we got nabbed."

He smiled helplessly. "Bra swapping! What a way to communicate?" He cleared his throat. "Okay, thank you. Now, I have to go contact...plus one."

She snickered. "Plus one," she said grinning. "Much more complimentary than anything I came up with."

Bates frowned and opened his mouth to ask. He closed his mouth and eyes. "I don't want to know."

"Hey!" She gave him a concerned look. "When am I going to get shipped back to Langley? Did you want me to do rehab... here?"

He smiled. "Don't worry. We'll get you back to Virginia as

soon as we possibly can. You just went through major surgery and you're pregnant. You're still a complete invalid. I'll check on all things possible…and get you back to the States when it is feasible."

"Okay," she sighed.

21

One of the KGB officers was sitting at his desk looking over documents that he had read several dozen times before. There was nothing new in any of them that gave him the slightest clue as to what had happened to 44021 and 98174. His best hope was that they had frozen to death, somewhere in the tundra.

An Aide came walking in with a sickened look on his face. "Comrade, I think…that we may have found…44021 and 98174!"

"Dead, I hope," he said with a tentative smile.

"No, Sir! I just received the transcript of an intercepted radio message. It came from an office in Cheb, Czechoslovakia."

"That's crazy! How could they have made it there? Finland or Turkey would have been a much better choice."

"Comrade, it came from Czechoslovakia. The message states that an American Army patrol was clearing a road that is close to the border, the morning after a fierce, blinding blizzard. They came upon a man, pulling a sled. The strange man spoke with an American accent, even though he was dressed as a Russian soldier. They claimed that the sled that he was pulling…had an injured woman on it. They didn't want to pick the two up…until the man shot out a rearview mirror and forced them, at gunpoint, to take him…and the injured woman…to the nearest military hospital."

He felt sick. All of those puzzling reports about a single Soviet military man pulling a sled. From Moscow to Minsk. From

Minsk to Krakow. From Krakow to Prague, to Cheb and then – silence. Now, a radio transmission, intercepted from the other side, told of this same man – with the sled. He nearly fell out of his chair.

"Are you feeling sick, Comrade? Do you think that it is possible that this was the couple that we were looking for? All of that time…and she was laying there…injured…on the sled. Could it possibly be them?"

"I don't know. We may have been following their trail…all the way…and did not realize that it was them…because SHE was hidden from our sight. We didn't know that she was injured to the point where she could not walk. He dragged her…and we could not see her…on the sled…and all of this time…we knew…exactly where they were…every step of the way."

With eyes wide with fear the Aide slowly walked up to the desk. "Those reports? The ones about…the lone man…with a sled? Again, Comrade, could that have really…been *them*…all along?"

He hung his head. "Is there anything in this new report that specifically says anything about the…identity of either one?"

"Yes, Comrade, the report clearly states…that the name of the man is Sergeant Bradley F. Dooley…or at least that is who he claimed to be."

He leaned his head back, agonizing over the possibilities. "Does it say anything about…the woman?"

"Yes, Comrade, she is called…Captain Marie Walker."

"Give me the report!" It was handed to him. He read it three times. "There is nothing in here…that tells how…or where they crossed over." He looked up confused. "The radio transmission was the morning after a terribly strong blizzard..." He stood up looking at the page in horror. "...a blizzard...that caused a complete white out! Zero visibility!"

"Comrade, Sir, the fence is still electrified. How could they have possibly...crossed the minefield...and an electrified fence... even in a storm?"

He flopped back down in his chair. "I don't know. But somehow...they did. She may have been injured...but she was not too injured to...crawl...over or under...or through the fence."

"Again, Comrade...where?"

He looked up angrily. "If I knew that...I could have done something about it." He sighed. "Start inspecting the fence...all along the border between...West Germany and Czechoslovakia. Do thorough inspections around Cheb. If they crossed...on that border...there might be a clue somewhere."

"Comrade, Sir, in order to check the entire border, it will take some time!"

"Then the sooner it is started, the sooner we will get the information."

"Yes, Comrade. Uh...Comrade, should I report this to headquarters?"

"ARE YOU INSANE? If they get word that...we allowed those two spies to slip right through our hands...even though they were spotted...several times...between Moscow and Cheb, what do you think would happen to us?"

He cleared his throat and then swallowed hard. "We… would be the ones who would be sent…to a gulag…somewhere in Siberia."

With a nauseous look on his face he nodded. "How badly do you want that to happen? We would be sent there for life…either as a guard or…maybe even as a prisoner."

The Aide wandered out of the office muttering. "I keep my mouth shut. Moscow is bad enough. Sometimes I get to go to Odessa. That is not bad. Siberia…is very bad."

After the Aide was gone he started looking at all of the reports on the sighting of a man pulling a sled. He sequenced them according to date. He wanted to throw up. After getting all of them lined up, there were sixty-one sightings that showed the line of travel. From the area eleven kilometers outside of Moscow to Minsk. From Minsk to Krakow. From Krakow to Prague – to Cheb.

He walked over to his fireplace and threw the reports in. He watched as the flames slowly devoured the reports. He hoped that these were the only copies of the reports and that no one else had kept a copy. If they did, his career was over.

He had been believing the propaganda reports. Americans are not able to do any form of physical labor other than short sprints. No American could possibly outdo a Russian in a long distance physical endurance competition. The propaganda was obviously false. This American had done it.

22

Bradley was awakened by someone kicking his feet. He looked up through the haze of just waking up. A tall man was standing near the foot of the bed. The man was wearing a heavy parka. He had very dark eyes and closely trimmed brown hair. He appeared to have somewhat of a permanent scowl on his face. Bradley rubbed the sleep out of his eyes and looked a little closer at the tall man. He had a blue flight cap on, with a silver lining and an eagle. Bradley jumped up to attention.

The Colonel stared angrily at Bradley. "Just where and how did you get hold of my name?"

Bradley was momentarily confused. He stammered a little. "Who...are you...Sir?"

The Colonel leaned down with his face close to Bradley. "Colonel Samuel Bates! Now, how did you get my name?"

Bradley stood a little taller at attention. "Sir! I saw your name on a phony certificate of marriage that was handed to me by a woman who said that she was my wife. Sir!"

Bates looked up at the ceiling. He closed his eyes and snickered. He shook his head and sat down on the bed. "Sit down, son."

"Sir, is that an order?"

Bates looked up disgusted. "Sit down, smart-alec!"

Bradley complied – a little grudgingly.

Bates snickered again. "I must be careful where I put my signature, in the future."

Bradley looked suspiciously at Bates. "Sir, uh…do you know…what the heck is going on here?"

Bates looked at Bradley and smiled. "I'm the one who sent you on that little vacation…well, not you…I sent her. She grabbed you and brought you along…for whatever reason she did."

"But why, Sir? Is it possible for me to find out what that horrid trek through hell was for?"

Bates looked around. "I'll tell you what I can – but not here."

"Why not here, Sir?"

"It's not a secure area."

"Well, Sir, I don't have much of a choice as to where I can go."

Bates nodded. He stood up, went to the cell door and hollered: "Hey, who's in charge of this zoo?"

An Air Force Staff Sergeant came around a corner looking somewhat insulted. "I'm the one, currently on duty, Sir. What is it that you want?"

"First, I want out of this cell, second, I'm taking Sergeant Dooley with me."

"I can't let you take him without authorization, Sir."

Bates sighed. "Who's your Commanding Officer?"

"That would be Lieutenant Colonel Pierce, Sir."

"Fine, Sergeant, call him."

"I can't right now..."

"That's an order!" shouted Bates angrily.

The Sergeant closed his eyes and raised his eyebrows. "Yes, Sir," he said quietly.

He opened the door for Bates and both of them went back around the corner. Bradley laid back down on the bed to wait. He yawned and decided to get a little more sleep. It was wonderful not having to get up and look for rabbits...that you were going to eat... raw...breakfast, lunch and dinner. It was wonderful having the meal brought to him. It was warm and there were vegetables and milk and maybe sometimes there was some apple pie or peach cobbler. He really did not mind being in this prison cell. No worries, no responsibilities, no cold snow – no raw rabbit.

At noon, they brought him a meal. It consisted of chicken breast, peas and mashed potatoes, along with another pint of milk. He ate slowly, once again relishing the taste of a cooked meal.

"How can you eat that slop?" said the guard. "Ain't you got no pride in what you eat? Don't you know what good food is?"

Bradley stopped chewing and just stared back with a dull look.

The guard looked a little uncomfortable at the gaze. He walked away, shaking his head.

Bradley refused to give that man the satisfaction of *why*. Bates had said that the area was not secure enough to talk about what had happened, so maybe he should keep his mouth shut about all of it…for now.

Shortly after lunch was finished, Bates came back with Lt. Col. Pierce.

"Get ready," said Bates. "We're leaving."

"If you don't mind my asking, Sir," said Bradley, "where are we going?"

"Ramstein Air Base," said Bates.

Pierce looked around confused. "Excuse me, Colonel, but where are the guards? Aren't you going to need some kind of escort to keep this man in line?"

Bates looked a little impatient. "What's he done that I should be afraid of him? I mean he hasn't given any of your men here any guff. Why should I fear anything from him?"

"He shot at the men on the perimeter road, Sir," said Pierce angrily.

Bates sighed. He smiled at Pierce. "You don't have the whole story, do you?"

Pierce shrugged. "All right, Colonel, what am I missing?"

"First of all, Dooley and his colleague were there with authorization, my authorization. Don't ask why because it's on a need to know basis. Second, when he flagged down that truck, it was because his colleague was badly hurt with a head injury and he was trying to expedite her movement to a hospital. Those two idiots in the truck decided that they didn't want to stop and pick Dooley and the injured party up, because they would have to do some extra paperwork. So, they pulled away after telling Dooley to get out of the ten klick zone before they would pick him and the injured party up. Now! Consider! If you had just gone through a rather lengthy, arduous mission, your colleague is injured, they have a vehicle, they refuse to pick you and your friend up, and they drive away... laughing! You have a gun with you...what would you do? He was simply trying to get some badly needed medical attention for his colleague and he was reminding those two morons, at gunpoint, that they were shirking their duty. Now...who was in the wrong? Instead of putting him in jail, someone should be scolding those two shirkers, regarding *dereliction of duty*, not this man for *forcing* them to do their duty."

Pierce was looking at Bates with a consternation on his face. "Can this be corroborated?"

Bates smiled. "I said she was injured. She was *not* deaf. She heard every word that was said, but couldn't do a thing about it...because of her head injury." He stopped to take a breath. "This man and the Captain, were doing what I ordered them to do. Now that they have completed the task that I gave them, I have to take Sergeant Dooley back to Ramstein for a debriefing. Dooley did add that little bonus at the end, reminding two idiots, that they had an obligation to do their assigned tasks. As a result of him firing that shot, he got the Captain some desperately needed medical attention. Now, what criminal act are you going to charge him with, when he was obeying orders, my orders, as well as trying to get medical aid for the Captain? What are the charges...forcing two shirkers to comply with regulations?"

Pierce looked at Bradley. "When you fired that shot, you blew out his rearview mirror. What were you aiming at, when you fired that shot?"

"The rearview mirror," said Bradley flatly.

"You're that good a marksman?"

"You want me to prove it to you, Sir?"

Pierce sighed. "No, that won't be necessary. I've got enough busted mirrors in my motor pool…because of some idiot, misjudging distance. I can't spare any…for that." He looked at Bates. "All right Colonel, if you'll sign for him…"

Bates immediately had a pen in his hand, ready to sign anything, anywhere.

Pierce pointed towards his office. "The paperwork is in my office."

Bates raised his eyebrows. "Can we take him with us, so I don't have to come back to get him?"

Pierce cleared his throat. "My guess, Sir, is that you won't be needing any handcuffs or ankle shackles…or guards."

"No, I won't," said Bates evenly.

Pierce gave a signal to a guard who unlocked the cell door without comment.

The drive to Ramstein was very quiet. Bates told Dooley that the driver did not have the *need to know*, so there were no questions in the car. There was very little that the two had in common, so there was no small talk of any kind. While Bradley had numerous questions about what he was supposed to have been doing and why, he could not ask anything until they reached this *secure location*.

What had happened to Marie? He had no idea what was going on with her. He was sure that she was in good hands. He wondered why he should care. She had used him. She had pulled him into something that he was not trained for and he had been there for...what?

Bradley was nodding off from boredom when they reached the main gate of Ramstein AB...and drove right on by. He frowned and looked around in bewilderment. They drove to a fenced in compound that was close to the base. There was a guard at the gate, wearing an unfamiliar uniform. Bates and the driver had to show their ID card along with some other credential. Bates vouched for Bradley and without any reaction the guard waved them through. Bradley was even more confused over the fact that the guard had not saluted *Colonel* Bates.

They pulled around to the back of a very large building, where Bradley was a little surprised to see an armed escort. He got out of the car and immediately had a guard on either side of him, with one behind him as well. They headed for a guarded entrance, where again, they had to show credentials. This new stop also had a cipher lock, next to the door. As soon as they got in, Bates and all of the escorts hung red badges on their shirt pockets. Bradley was handed a yellow badge by one of the escorts. He took a quick look at it. All that was on it was one word in red: "Visitor".

They went through a small foyer to another door with a cipher lock. A code was fed in, the door clicked and one of the escorts pushed it open. They went through the door into a hallway, where there were a lot of open doors and a few people in suits standing around talking. Immediately the escort behind Bradley started hollering: "Yellow badge in the area, secure your area!" Doors were being shut as they walked by and conversations were abruptly halted as everyone turned and stared at Dooley. He began to understand what it felt like to be a leper.

They went to an elevator. Bates pushed the call button and they waited in silence. When the door opened, they walked in and Bates had to punch in another code on a cipher lock inside the elevator.

Bates turned to Bradley and smiled. "Do you need something to eat? I know I do."

Bradley was rather confused at all of this security, however, he tried not to show his concern. "Sir, what I need right now, is a latrine break. We were in that car for…I don't know how long. I'd rather find a commode and get rid of something…before I try to fill up again."

Bates simply nodded to the escorts. One of them nodded back. As soon as the elevator door opened up on the fifth floor, the rear escort started up again. "Yellow badge in the area, secure your area!"

They escorted him to the latrine. When they arrived the escort stuck his head inside and shouted again. "Yellow badge in the area, secure your area!" Bradley was allowed to enter by himself, seeing as how no one else was in there at the time. He walked into a stall, dropped his pants and sat down. "Hey loudmouth," he whispered. "What do they need to secure in a crapper?"

He smiled. The sheer pleasure of being able to sit, without having to worry about holding onto a branch to keep from falling down in the cold snow (as well as your own feces) was wonderful. He felt that he would never complain about the condition of any commode after his grueling quest. He was thinking of spending an hour or two here, however...the guards might wonder. He finished his constitutionals, did the necessary paperwork, got dressed, washed his hands and headed out.

"Yellow badge in the area, secure your area!"

Bradley was really beginning to hate that sound. They escorted him into a snack bar in the center of the building and when the "Yellow Badge" was sounded, the room became very quiet and all eyes seemed to be on him. As he went up to get food he heard a few conversations start up again – something about a recent hockey game and a few things about a football game that had taken place, very early in the season.

He picked up a tray and started sliding it down the rail looking at the choices. He had all kinds of choices in front of him: Veal, chicken, and some kind of brown lump. There were a few hamburger patties sizzling on a grill in the back. Mashed potatoes, green beans, peas and carrots, and some cooked broccoli. He decided on a club sandwich that seemed to be calling to him. He grabbed some extra chips to go with the sandwich. In between the apple pie and cherry pie, there was a piece of pecan pie that was screaming to be taken by him and nearly brought tears of joy to his eyes. He also got something that he had not seen since Marie grabbed him out of his normal life...a large soda. Then he saw the cash register. Oops! How was he going to pay for this?

Before he could really get too worried about payment, the cashier spoke up: "Hey, are that Sergeant Dooley?"

"Uh...yeah...why?"

"Bates is paying for your food. He left me a sawbuck to pay and said that you'd bring the change back to him.

"Right!" 'Fair enough,' thought Bradley.

The cashier rang it up and put the change and a receipt on Bradley's tray. He gave the man a quick smile and thanks and then was escorted by "Loudmouth" and the other two escorts to another interrogation room.

Bates was sitting at a table in the room, just finishing his meal. Bradley snapped to attention – tray still in hand. Bates smiled. "You can forget those formalities in here." He motioned to another chair by the table. "Sit down...eat...relax." He looked at the escorts. "You can wait outside."

Bradley wondered just what was going to happen in here (and for how long). He sat down picked up all of the money, handed it with the receipt to Bates. He then started that slow gratifying pleasure of eating something other than raw rabbit.

Bates took the change and put it in his pocket. He barely glanced at the receipt. He leaned back in his chair and wiped his mouth. "We need for you to tell us everything that happened to you on your tour behind the iron curtain. We need you to tell us – a day-by-day account – if you can remember. If you can't remember day-by-day then anything that you came across and that sticks out in your mind because of it being an anomaly or unique or...what ever happened to make you remember that particular tidbit of information. Anything that you can tell us will be greatly appreciated."

"Will I have to be here, the whole time, Sir?"

"The mission was *Top Secret*, so...yes. This is one of the few places that you can talk about it and you are allowed in. We'll have some place else that you can go to sleep...and eat."

Bradley took a gulp of the soda. It had been so long since he had tasted a carbonated drink that it almost felt like it was burning his mouth. "Where do you want me to start, Sir?"

Bates smiled. "I'm not the one conducting the debriefing. Members of my staff will be discussing the trip with you."

"Have you heard anything about Marie, Sir...I mean, the Captain? I was wondering just exactly what happened to her and how she's doing."

Bates looked lost in thought for a few moments. He leaned forward and sighed. "According to the doctors, she suffered some kind of brain damage. She had a very nasty skull fracture, that did some natural healing on its own, while you were pulling her along. They will probably have to replace a portion of her skull with a metal plate. They had to get inside her brain box and find out just exactly what damage they could find and repair. The rest of her body seems to be, very much, unaffected...other than bed sores and a touch of diaper rash."

Bradley felt a little guilty. "I did what I could for her, Sir. She was totally helpless and I just don't have any kind of…training for handling or caring for a complete invalid."

Bates chuckled. "No one is going to condemn you for your lack of medical knowledge. When you look at the big picture, you did a very good job of taking care of her…in spite of any ignorance you may have on medical procedures."

"What about the vitamin deficiency, Sir?"

That one surprised Bates completely. He closed his eyes for a moment, with his mouth hanging wide open. He frowned. "Uh… deficiency…vitamin…what?"

"I've seen pictures of some of those starving children in Africa who are suffering badly, from malnutrition. Their stomachs are swollen so large that it looks like their stomach is over half of their body weight. Her stomach started swelling during the last part of the trip…no matter how much food I gave her. I didn't seem to help the problem, so I was wondering: Just exactly what happened with her health issue?"

Bates leaned back and cleared his throat. "I'll definitely have to check in on that." He quietly wondered about the pregnancy that she had mentioned to him. He pondered the thought – deficiency or pregnancy? That was something he was going to go back and check on.

A young man came in and took the food trays away. Bradley and Bates sat there looking at each other for a few minutes when the door opened up and three men came into the room. Bradley saw that all three men were Majors wearing Air Force uniforms and he snapped to attention.

"We can dispense with that for the time being," said Bates. "I need you to give these men a full briefing on what you did, where, how and anything else you can think of on your trip through and out of Russia."

Bradley relaxed and smiled. He noticed that none of the three Majors was wearing a name tag. He thought that this was very strange – for a few minutes. After what he had been through, nothing else could ever be that strange again.

23

The three Majors kept at Bradley – day after day after day. They wanted to know how many days he had traveled. They wanted to know how often he had stopped and snared rabbits. They wanted to know how many rabbits. They wanted to know how many rabid animals he had come across and when. They wanted to know how many wolves he had fed with one of his live rabbits. They wanted to know where the crash had taken place. They wanted to know how many people had died in the crash. They wanted to know where he had come up with the idea of using the inner tubes. They wanted to know what gave him the idea of sliding across the ice over a minefield. They wanted to know how many rivers he had crossed, as well as how many were frozen over and how many times he had stolen a boat to cross. They wanted to know what unit it was that had been involved in that winter patrol as well as how many men and trucks were involved. They wanted to know how he had devised the idea to use the blanket of coats and rubber on the fence. They wanted to know where he had learned how to set up a snare. They wanted to know just how good a marksman he really was. They wanted to know…they wanted to know…they wanted to know.

They were not very satisfied with the fact that he had no clue how many days he had traveled. They were unsatisfied with the fact that he had no idea where the crash had taken place. They were unsatisfied with his off-the-cuff idea of using inner tubes. They were unsatisfied with the fact that he did not know which military unit it was that bivouacked near him that night. They were unsatisfied with how and where he had crossed the fence.

Bradley was getting very frustrated. He had been asked the same questions, over and over and over and over and over. He could not understand why they were not happy with the same answer for the same question each time they repeated the question.

They never told him their names. The only thing he could do was (in his mind) call them Blonde, Brunette and Baldy.

One of the very few satisfying moments for Bradley was when Baldy got slapped in the face by a snare when it was sprung. They had asked him to show how he had set the snares. He showed them. Baldy got too close as the demonstration was done. Baldy might have a very ugly scar, for the rest of his life, on his forehead. None of the Majors were amused, however, Bradley got a good long giggle out of the incident.

They finally got the message that he had no clue as to the exact location of the crash. They finally got the message that he had no clue as to how many days he was traveling. They finally got the message that he had no clue as to the fact that he did not know his exact route. They finally got the message that he had learned from a buddy in Georgia, as to how to set a snare. They finally got the message that he had only stolen one boat, because all the other rivers were not quite as wide and they were frozen over when he got to them. They finally got the message that he had no clue as to which unit it was that camped out that night, because he could not speak, read or write Russian. They finally got the message that he had learned about how rubber was not a conductor, but it was an excellent insulator, in shop class in high school.

Day after day he was interrogated about every tiny detail of the journey from Moscow to Hof Air Base. Bradley was finally fed up with this entire ordeal. He decided to come up with one pat answer. "The answer to that question is still the same as it was the last dozen times that you asked that question." No matter what question they asked him he kept repeating the same line.

Apparently they finally got the message. He was taken to the interrogation room one more time. No one showed up for over an hour. Finally when the door did open, it was not one of the three Majors. Instead a Captain and a civilian walked in. Bradley snapped to attention when he saw this new Captain. 'Great,' he thought. 'A new officer that I'm *not* familiar with.'

The Captain was a tall slender woman with very dark hair and eyes. She smiled and told him to relax. "I'm Captain Janice Card and my colleague is Special Agent Frank Dixon of the FBI."

Bradley looked at Dixon. The man was a little shorter than Capt. Card and had very thin brown hair on the top of his head. He wore a somewhat drab looking blue suit (at least it was not gray).

Bradley sat there waiting for the other shoe to drop. He had gone through all kinds of boring questioning from the Majors – what now?

Dixon placed a rather large suitcase on the table. He opened it and pulled out three rather large 3-ring binders. "These are the reports from the men who have been debriefing you over the last six weeks. We learned a lot of interesting things from your little quest across Russia...to here."

"Six weeks?" Bradley was ready to be sick. He had lost

complete track of time with all of the repetitious questions. Six long, boring weeks. His shoulders slouched and his chin hit his chest.

Captain Card looked a little concerned. "Is there something wrong?"

Bradley looked up at her dull-eyed. "Six weeks of questions. Two and a half months of running around behind the iron curtain. A month of some rather…silly preparations prior to taking the trip. Five months out of my life and I still am not sure what I was doing. What could possibly be wrong Ma'am?" He sat back in his chair and looked at the ceiling while shaking his head.

"Yes, well sometimes, these thing do take a little time," said the Captain.

"Now it's over," said Dixon. "We now have a form that we need you to look over and sign. Before you look it over, I will give you the short version: We are still a little bewildered at how you were able to get back to West Germany without being caught. It makes for some very interesting reading for the people who study these kind of things. You, however, are not allowed to be one of those people who get to read it."

Bradley raised his eyebrows, perplexed. He then snorted and rolled his eyes.

Card looked a little angry. "What was that for?"

He chuckled. "I'm not allowed to read…what happened to me over the last five months. I am practically the one who wrote that wretched thing."

She looked away embarrassed. "Yes, but, now you have to forget it."

"Once you leave this room," continued Dixon. "You will not be allowed to discuss this episode with anyone, at any time, or anywhere. This report is going to be classified *Top Secret* and that is final."

"I wouldn't discuss it with anyone anyway," said Bradley flatly.

Card looked puzzled now. "Why do *you* want to keep it such a secret?"

"Captain...no one would believe it. I'd be called a liar and an idiot for coming up with such a hare-brained tall tale. I'd just rather forget the whole crappy thing."

"Good," said Dixon with a smile. He slid the paper toward Bradley. "Now, read it and sign it, please."

"What exactly is it, again?"

"It's a document stating that you are to keep your mouth shut about the affair. If you ever do discuss it...after signing, you can be court-martialed for insubordination and improper disclosure of classified material...among other things. You could end up in jail for a long, long time."

Bradley took his sweet time reading the document. After reading it for the fourth time he picked up the pen and signed.

Dixon put the three binders in the suitcase along with the document that Bradley signed. He picked up the suitcase and left the room.

Card smiled. "Was there anything else that you need…that you can think of?"

Bradley shook his head. "Other than out of here…and fifty bucks worth of beer…no, Ma'am. I can't think of a thing."

24

Bradley finally got back to his unit at Rhein Main. His original room in the barracks was now occupied by someone else, so he was assigned to a new room. He had to put up with a very loquacious new roommate – Airman First Class Jonathan Hopper. Hopper was a young, pimple faced loudmouth and he was from Michigan. He bored Bradley to tears with his stories about Kalamazoo and the surrounding area and how it was so much nicer in Michigan than it was in Germany.

At work, Bradley was plagued with questions about where he had been and what he had done. Instead of telling them that he was not allowed to divulge any information, he simply told them that they would not believe him, so there was no point in telling them anything. He knew that if he told them that it had been a classified mission, all they would do was hound and harass him for more information…or call him a liar.

After several days, back on the job, he was called to his Squadron Commander's office – NOW! He headed to the orderly room, with some concern on his mind. Was Lt. Col. Fowler going to start asking questions as well? Was there some problem with work? Was there some new deployment that would pull him out on some other idiotic mission to – wherever?

He walked into the Orderly Room and looked around. He was confused and fearful when he saw…three Majors: Blonde, Brunette and Baldy. This time, however, they were wearing name tags. Bradley took a quick glance at their name tags, rolled his eyes and nearly gagged. – Smith, Jones and Johnson. What was the possibility that those were their real names? NONE! Bradley shook his head and sighed. Still more silly intrigue.

Baldy (or rather Major Johnson) stood up and walked towards Bradley, with a smile on his face. He stuck out his hand to give a friendly handshake. "Well, it's good to see you again, Sergeant Dooley."

Bradley kept a straight face, shook Johnson's hand and simply gave an acknowledging: "Sir." 'It's not good to see you… or either one of those other goons,' he thought. 'I didn't like it then and I don't like it any more now.'

The other two Majors walked up. "Since you're here, I guess it's time to go see your Commanding Officer," said Baldy.

Brunette (or rather Major Jones) looked at a young Sergeant sitting at a nearby desk. "Is your Commander available at this time?"

She smiled. "He's itching to find out what's going on, Sir. Go right on in."

Major Johnson signaled for Dooley to lead the way. Bradley was a little surprised at this breach of etiquette, but he decided not to comment on it at all. He merely walked in ahead of the three Majors.

When they walked in, Lt. Col. Fowler was off to the side of his office pouring himself a cup of coffee. He put his mug down and walked towards the Majors, looking them up and down. Fowler was a very tall man. He towered over all four of the other men in the room. He was lean and was a stickler for appearance. He could quote any portion of the Air Force Dress Code from memory. He was also the type that got a haircut once a week, whether he needed it or not. "Gentlemen," he said cordially. "Let's have a sit down and discuss...what we are allowed to discuss."

Blonde (or rather Major Smith) was the last one to enter the room and closed the door behind him.

Fowler frowned. "Is that necessary? Usually the only time I do that...I'm getting ready to ream someone out for...just about anything."

"I'm afraid so, Sir," said Major Smith. "This was a classified mission that your man was on."

Fowler shrugged, scratched his head and looked around the room. "All right, again, let's discuss...whatever we can discuss. I would like to know whatever I can about this situation and if there is anything else that might affect one of my troops. So, gentlemen, have a seat and let's find out what we can."

After everyone was seated Major Johnson started talking. "I know that it is a little frustrating being told that you don't have the need to know about Dooley's activities over the last few months."

Fowler raised his eyebrows. "*Little* frustrating? Did I hear you say *little*? Little frustrating is a gargantuan understatement. Monumental pain right between the butt cheeks is much closer to the truth...but still not quite there."

Johnson cleared his throat and smiled. "All right, Sir, *very* frustrating. Unfortunately, it can't be helped. The only thing that I can tell you is some of the aftermath."

"I can hardly wait," said Fowler sarcastically as he rolled his eyes.

"Yes," said Johnson with a bit of a strained smile. "Prior to us getting your Sergeant, I understand that he had a problem with aerobics testing. I will tell you that what he did, during his time with us, we will enter it into his records that he definitely passed his aerobics."

Fowler looked up and contemplated. "Good news," he said flatly. "Go on."

Major Jones place a briefcase on his lap, opened it and pulled out a small flat blue box. "During his time with us, your Sergeant performed admirably. As a result, I have the honor or presenting him with this. Unfortunately, the comments that go with it are sealed… as well."

Fowler took the box. He sniffed and then opened it. A look of total shock went across his face. He looked at each one of the Majors as if he were trying to glean something from their expressions. "Are you serious?" He looked back down at the contents of the box. "You are telling me that…an E-4 has done something to warrant being a recipient of the Meritorious Service Medal?" He closed his eyes and shook his head. "The Air Force Commendation Medal…I might understand, but…the MSM?"

All three Majors nodded while smiling.

"Sir, we can't tell you everything," said Johnson. "What

I can tell you is that, because of his actions, the mission was accomplished…in a manner that we never expected." He looked up in contemplation. "It was…very unique." He looked back at Fowler and smiled. "And he did save a colleagues life. If we could have, we would have gone to the Airman's Medal, but…that was not approved, unfortunately."

Fowler was sitting there in stunned silence. He turned to Bradley, opened the box up again and handed it to Bradley. "Congratulations, Sergeant Dooley! Well done! I only wish I knew exactly what it was that you did. That way I could be a little more sincere about this whole thing."

Bradley accepted the box with a nervous smile on his face. "Thank you, Sir." He tried to think of something else, but could not so he just left it alone.

Fowler turned back to the Majors. "Is there anything else that I can be informed of?"

"Yes," said Major Smith with a big smile. "Seeing as how Sergeant Dooley was, unavoidably not allowed to test for promotion…"

"What?" Again Fowler was looking at the Majors in shock. "Are you talking an automatic promotion?"

Major Smith smiled and nodded. "Yes, Sir. Because of circumstances beyond his control, at the beginning of the cycle, he will have the promotion line number – '1'. I do have a set here…"

Fowler raised his hands for Smith to stop. "I'm aware of the custom, Major. I'm well prepared for it." With that he reached down to one of the lower drawers in his desk. He shuffled through a few things and pulled something out. He looked at the items cupped in his huge hands, looked at Bradley and smiled. He stood up, which made everyone else stand up, strode purposefully towards Bradley. Bradley was standing there with some surprise on his face as well.

"Again, congratulations, Staff Sergeant *Selectee* Dooley. As is the usual custom, I, your Squadron Commanding Officer, present you with your first set of Staff Sergeant Chevrons."

Bradley took the chevrons with shaky hands. He shook Fowler's hand and swallowed hard. "Th-thank you, Sir." He cleared his throat and stared at the chevrons, somewhat confused. He saluted Fowler, who returned the salute.

"Now, Sir," said Johnson. "We need to borrow Sergeant Dooley for a little while."

Fowler glared at Johnson. "How many months, this time?"

Johnson held up his hands and chuckled. "We are talking hours this time, Sir. Definitely not months…not this time."

"Good!" Fowler cleared his throat. "For a moment there, I thought that I might have to hand him some Technical Sergeant chevrons upon his next return…with a further awarding of the Airman's Medal…or even the Air Force Medal of Honor."

"Oh no, Sir," said Johnson. "Just hours. Our Commander wants to have a quick chat with him about something else."

Fowler stood there akimbo looking at Bradley. "Well, I found out…nothing about what you did. I did find out that whatever you did – you did a whale of a good job. I understand the necessity of keeping classified information a secret, but, there are times that I just don't like it." He looked up at nothing in particular. "This afternoon, after work, I am going to go home, change into my sweat suit, go the gym and beat the unholy *crap* out of a punching bag. I hope that that will help relieve a little of this confounded frustration." He turned to the three Majors. "Is there anything else?"

All three Majors shook their heads smiling.

"Well, have a nice day and a safe trip...to wherever it is that you're going." He looked at Bradley. "Again...congratulations for the...medal and the promotion. Also, thank you for doing a good job and setting a fine example...for whatever you did."

25

Bradley got another ride in a staff car. This ride was not near as long as the one he had taken before. He was expecting to go to Ramstein, or at least next to the base, to meet with Col. Bates. Instead they went to the Rhein Main AB Officers Billeting. Bradley was a little confused at first but figured that this Bates character could go anywhere or do anything at any time that he wanted and who would question it.

Bradley followed Maj. Johnson up a flight of stairs, down a hallway and was suddenly very confused when he realized that Smith and Jones were not with them anymore and he had not been aware of their departure until Johnson stopped at a door and knocked. Bradley recognized that deep voice when the expected: "Who's there?" inquiry came from the other side.

"Johnson and Dooley," said the Major.

"Send him in," said Bates.

Johnson looked at Bradley and smiled. "Go ahead."

Bradley opened the door, walked in and saw Bates sitting in an overstuffed chair, dressed very casually. Bates gave Bradley a questioning look. "Are you going to close the door?"

Bradley turned and was a little startled to find that Johnson had vacated the area without making a sound. He nervously cleared his throat and closed the door. He looked back at Bates. "What now, Sir?"

"You probably have a few unanswered questions and so do I. Since I am the only one that you can talk with, regarding the mission, I set up this little chat."

"Weren't all the questions answered when those goons of yours were torturing me, Sir?"

Bates got a somewhat angered look on his face. "My *staff* was *debriefing* you. We don't have goons...and torture is not authorized...by the Geneva Convention and the Regulations in the Uniform Code of Military Justice."

Bradley wanted desperately to repeat the *goons* and *torture*, however, he knew that he could never win the argument, so he let it be – for the moment. "Why did she need me to go along? What possible good could I have done on that silly...whatever it was? All I did was go along and look stupid."

Bates rubbed his forehead. "When this thing started, I gave her and a few others a free ticket on how to carry out the mission. We had received some very disturbing information from behind the iron curtain. It sounded as if the entire free world was at risk. We had to get someone in there and find out if there was any truth to the information."

"So we were never there looking for one specific individual?"

"Uh...no! She was sent there to investigate and find out if the information had any credibility."

Bradley clenched his teeth. "So we were always scheduled to go to Russia?"

Bates looked a little confused. "*Yes*! What kind of a cock

and bull story did she give you?"

"She said that she and I were supposed to be a diversion. You were looking for a certain individual and once he was found, we go in and stay in the immediate vicinity. That guy knew her and would, supposedly be confused, because he did NOT know me. He would try to find out who I was and supposedly stay in the area until he found out. Meanwhile, you guys are looking at him, following him, learning about him, while he is looking at me."

Bates had a look of total bewilderment. "Why would she give you a line like that?"

Bradley closed his eyes and gritted his teeth. "You just answered that question, Sir."

"I did?" he said incredulously.

"Yes, Sir."

Bates shook his head and his shoulders sagged. "Well then you're going to have to explain it to me...because you just lost me."

Bradley rolled his eyes. "DIVERSION! That's what she said we were going to be. The main lie was that the diversion was not WE, the diversion was ME! The *guy* we were supposed to confuse was not a guy, it was the whole rotten KGB. That's why they didn't torture me in the same room where they strip searched her. They did a little soft-soap on me and were planning to do something really nasty, once we got to...wherever it was we were headed to, when the crash happened."

Bates sighed. "You seem to have thought this through pretty well, but you lost me a little somewhere in the story line. Why did she take you along?"

"That stinkin' broad was using ME as a decoy. She was going to do her mission stuff and if there was trouble, she was going to try to lay it all on me, while she escaped. I was a little part of a diversion and a major part scapegoat. While the KGB was questioning me, she would make her escape good, I can't tell them anything of any value and I end up in a gulag for the next thirty or forty years."

Bates pursed his lips. "She IS definitely more of a gutter rat than I originally thought she was. So, where do you think it went wrong and she got caught as well?"

"I'd say that the KGB acted faster than she thought they would.'

Bates chuckled and nodded in agreement.

"What was the information that she was supposed to be looking for?"

Bates sighed. "Usually that's on a need to know basis. You don't need to know, but I think that you deserve to know." He looked off to the side contemplating and shook his head. He turned back to Bradley with a very serious look on his face. "The Russians started a massive rumor. This rumor said that they had some fancy new gizmo that could knock out *any* electrically run source of ours, at a distance of over 400 kilometers. Supposedly it was some system that they had been working on – at some secret location somewhere in Russia – and had now perfected it. So we had to find out the truth of this information. The whole blasted thing was a giant *red herring*. They set it up so that they could watch all entry points and capture as many western agents as they could. They knew that there would be a big influx of foreign agents, so they watched very carefully."

"So we were a couple of spooks, chasing a spook story, so another bunch of spooks could spook us out into the open and stick it to us good."

"I'm afraid so. If this is any consolation for you, she did get in touch with her contacts and they were able to get the true information back to us, before you two were caught. They just weren't able to get back to her in let her know, in time, that there was no more need for her...or you, to stay in Moscow any longer."

"Hip, hip, hooray," said Bradley sarcastically. "We overstayed our welcome."

"Yes. Well, that's that. Now to other things."

Bradley frowned. "What else is there? What else could I possibly need to know, or want to know about this whole mess?"

"While you were dragging her across Russia, she was a total invalid. The doctors at that Regional Medical Center in Frankfurt opened up her skull and found that she had suffered some kind of trauma and injury to the head. That injury put a large blood clot inside her brain box and that clot put pressure on the brain. That pressure greatly diminished certain messages to the voluntary muscles of the body and that is why she was so helpless. She could move...just not very much. Now, that they have removed that clot, she is now rehabilitating a lot of flaccid muscles, in order to get back to her *very* active lifestyle."

"So…that monster is okay."

Bates raised his eyebrows. "It will take a few months. She was inactive for two and a half months. You don't spring back from that kind of inactivity overnight."

He sighed in relief and smiled. "So I don't have any need to see her again."

Bates snickered. "There is the question of your marriage. The two of you are still legally married."

Bradley glared at Bates. "No we are NOT! There was nothing legal about that totally bogus marriage…Sir!"

"Maybe not *totally legal*, but there is a certain problem, growing larger at this moment."

Bradley was taken aback. "Huh? I don't understand what you're talking about. The only problem I have is that you claim that there's any legality to that so-called marriage."

"You said that you noticed that her stomach was getting bigger. That is not malnutrition - she's pregnant!" Bates let the information sink in a little while trying to read the scowl on Bradley's face.

Bradley stood there still angry and trying to control his breathing. "She said that she was on the pill – and even if she did get pregnant, it was not, and is not, my problem. I am not going to make it my problem. I don't consider that we were married, so that little bastard is not my concern at all. Her words – as well as mine, Sir! Also, you are the one who signed that phony marriage certificate. There is NOTHING legal about it."

Bares chuckled. "Believe it or not, I do have the authority to wed. Since I signed it, it is valid."

"Not in my opinion, Sir," said Bradley through clenched teeth.

"Well something is going to have to be done in order to properly care for that child."

"Not me! Her words: If she got pregnant, it was her problem, not mine."

Bates narrowed his eyes and glared at Bradley. "In less than a month and a half, your child is going to be born and you couldn't care less? Why? What kind of a man are you?"

Bradley was momentarily startled. "What did you say?"

"I asked you – what kind of a man are you?"

"No, Sir, before that."

Now Bates looked startled. "Before...uh...what?"

"Less than a month and a half? Is that what you said?"

"Yes, what difference does that make?"

"So, she is getting close to the end of, or has already gotten past seven months of her pregnancy...plus."

"Right...and...?"

"How long ago was it that I first met her, Colonel?"

"What? What has that got...?" Bates trailed off and looked a little confused as he did a few mental calculations.

"Right!" Bradley felt rather triumphant. "It was just over five months ago that I first met her. If she is past seven months...of her pregnancy...I am NOT the first one who got inside her. Someone else is the father...leaving me in the clear. Go back to her and find out who she was playing sticky-fingers with then. HE'S the father, not me."

Bates sat there quietly contemplating for several moments with his mouth hanging open. It was infuriating to think that he had made that kind of an error in calculations. Dooley was right. He was not the father and therefore not responsible. Bates would have to check with Wintergreen in order to see if she does know who the father really is. He finally looked up at Bradley, chuckled weakly, gave a guilty smile and quietly said: "Oops."

"So, now, you can take care of that phony baloney marriage?" Bradley insisted.

Bates sighed. "It really isn't that easy."

"Yes it is!" shouted Bradley.

Bates looked at Bradley in an accusing manner.

"...Sir," said Bradley just before he gulped.

"How am I supposed to just make that...validated...marriage disappear?"

"With the same crummy fountain pen you used to make it appear legal...Sir! If you have the capability of making it, then you have the capability of UN-making it."

Bates sighed. "Because of the baby, we snuck some documentation into the archives in South Carolina, that totally legalized your..." Bates shook his head. "Now, we have to go back and retrieve all of it. Do you see what you're doing here?"

Bradley put his hands over his face and groaned. He dropped his hands, looked and Bates and huffed. "Not my problem, Sir. When you snuck the stuff in there, all you did was make the problem worse. You didn't fix anything, you just busted it further." He folded his arms across his chest. "NOT my problem, Sir."

Bates cleared his throat and looked around dejectedly. "Yes, you are correct. It is not your problem. Is there anything else you want to bring up? I mean this is probably the last time that you will be able to talk about this situation to anyone...ever again."

Bradley looked up and considered for a moment. "Well, I was wondering about one rather strange turn of events. The whole time that I was dragging Marie – or whatever her name is – she was dull-eyed and slow to respond. She would answer my yes/no questions by blinking her eyes. She would eat, anything and everything I gave her. But...she just seemed distant. Then, as soon as I got her over the fence into West Germany...she just...all of a sudden...came alive. She showed emotion in her eyes and she seemed more alert. She seemed to react differently. I was wondering if somehow... when I got her across the fence, there was some kind of...I don't know. Some kind of miraculous healing?"

Bates snickered slightly. "No." He shook his head. "I talked to her about that situation. I asked her how she felt, during that trip. I mean what was going through her head as she was being dragged along? What was it that she felt when she was, all of a sudden, on the west side? No, she did not have any form of miracle healing or any form of revelation. Once you had her on the west side of the fence, she finally felt that she could actually survive the ordeal."

"What?" Bradley was totally confused. "I know that she was probably frustrated because of her inability to move, or even control her bodily functions. But…why all of a sudden did she think that she could not survive earlier? Did she think that she was going to die from her injuries or that I would leave her somewhere?"

"Cold sandwich," said Bates flatly.

Bradley sat there for a moment, expecting more. He looked around the room confused. He looked back at Bates. "What sandwich? Are we breaking for lunch? I mean what has that got to do with her coming alive emotionally?"

"When you were in school, did you ever hear about a certain tragic occurrence on the history of our nation – 'The Donner Party'?"

Bradley frowned and sat there with his lower jaw just hanging. "Yes, Sir, I do remember hearing about the Donner Party. What has that got to do with her emotions?"

"There is a certain…survival technique. This technique is taught to all field agents. Do what you have to do in order to survive. If you are in a situation where there are two or more agents…one of the agents is getting weak or sick…the stronger ones have a cold sandwich…if they cannot find any other form of nourishment."

Bradley stood there limp. He felt a wave of nausea come over him. He straightened up and shook his head while trying to think of something to say. He cleared his throat several times. He finally stopped moving and just stared at Bates.

"Whatever it takes," said Bate sternly. "You complete the

mission. If you have to eat your colleague – you do it! You do it one piece at a time...if you have to."

"Cannibalism?" Bradley felt even worse. "You are telling me that you resort to cannibalism, in order to...?"

"Whatever it takes! If you have any pride in completing the mission, you do whatever it takes."

"And she thought that I was..."

"She told me that she was praying that the abundance of rabbits did not cease. She knew that as long as there were rabbits, then she had a chance of surviving. She was still rather despondent, she appreciated being able to live another day...intact, but she is a highly trained field agent and she knows what can happen. She was the one who was helpless and so she would or could have been the cold sandwich."

"And she thought that this untrained schmuck of a non-professional field agent was going to turn her into...sushi...even though I didn't know about this...this horror?"

"Yes."

"Well, she must be pretty happy about the fact that I'm not a professional...cannibal."

"You could be."

"Huh?"

"You could be a very good field agent."

"Are you insane...Sir?"

"No, I'm just saying that the thought process that you went through, in order to complete the mission, showed marvelous intelligence, quick thinking, a great deal of intestinal fortitude and the ability to cope with and utilize what little you had at your disposal. You could be an outstanding field agent. That is the real reason I asked you to come here today. I was wondering if I could recruit you into the service."

Bradley had his hands up, palms out toward Bates, and shaking them back and forth. He started shaking his head as well, while a strange sound came out of his throat. He stopped the body movements and looked at Bates with horror on his face. "No, no, no, no, no, no, no. That'll never happen. When I was running across the Russian frontier, I used up a lot of punches on my 'dumb luck' card. I don't want to end up in a position – voluntarily – where I have to use all the rest of the card, plus I will never become a brain-dead...*cannibal*." His whole body shuddered with repulsion.

Bates smiled. "You say that now." He looked off to the side and picked up a business card. "I'll give you a phone number. You can call me whenever you change your mind." He held the card out to Bradley.

"I don't want that thing. I'm not gonna change my mind. I'd have to lose my mind in order to..." He shuddered in disgust again.

"Take the card and that's an order! You don't know. You could change your mind in a week, in a month, in a year – you never know."

Bradley took the card daintily between his index finger and thumb. He held it away at arm's length. He scowled at it. "I know!

I will never change my mind. If cannibalism is a normal part of your life...I don't want it – ever...Sir!"

Bates smiled again. "You say that now." He sniffed and his smile got bigger. "If you change your mind, you have my number." He picked up a phone near him, dialed a number and waited a few moments. "Yes, he's ready to go back now." He hung up the phone. "The driver, who is going to take you back, will be at the door in a few moments. You can leave now. I'll await your call."

"Right Colonel. Don't call me, I'll be avoiding calling you. It'll be one cold day in hell before I even think of calling you. Don't hold your breath...or rather *do* hold your breath...several times. Hold your breath until you have a stroke and then I won't have to put up with you, or call you, at all."

There was a knock on the door. Bradley decided to get out without any of the normal etiquette. He just wanted to leave as fast as he possibly could. The person at the door was the driver. Bradley departed with him with great haste. He could hardly wait until he got to the car and was escaping from this unholy horror...for good.

After Bradley departed, Smith, Jones and Johnson walked into the room where Bates was relaxing.

Johnson spoke up: "Do you actually think that he will call you?"

Bates looked up with a satisfied smile. "Yes, I do. I can usually read people very well. He is in shock right now. Once the shock wears off, he will realize that the escapade in Russia was the most fun that he has ever had in his boring, mundane existence. He will tire of the rut that he's in and he'll come crawling back."

The three men all looked very skeptical.

Jones chuckled. "Did you tell him…just how lucky he really was?"

Bates snickered. "No. When he calls back…I will. It's another punch on his dumb luck card that got used up."

Johnson looked confused. "What'd I miss?"

Bates cocked his head with another snicker. "The fence… where he jumped over the border. He accidentally stumbled on the one area where he could get away with what he did."

"You still lost me," said Johnson.

Smith huffed. "Haven't you been reading some of the updates? For years, the Russians have been rebuilding the fences and walls. They're trying to modernize and – if you can swallow their load of crap – *beautify* the fences and walls – as if anyone could figure out a way to beautify a prison. The area that Dooley came to was the last area that had not been updated yet. All the rest of the fences are three meters high, with razor wire on top, they're electrified and there are motion detectors. If he had gone eight kilometers north…or five kilometers south…he would have come across the new fence…and probably never have made it…unless he figured out a way to turn those bayonets into wire cutters."

Johnson sat there with his mouth open. "Oh…that report. I remember reading it, but, until now, I just didn't…think of how lucky he was…on his spot for…crossing. Wow! He really did use up a lot of dumb luck punches, didn't he?"

"He most certainly did," said Bates.

Jones looked doubtful. "And you really think that he would want to come back to us?"

Bates nodded with a big grin on his face.

Smith frowned. "How are you able to pinpoint his crossing location...so precisely?"

"Their Commanding Officer finally got those two negligent Army types to confess that they had seen...Wintergreen plus one and give a specific location as to where they picked them up," said Bates with a smirk. "It couldn't have possibly been very far from there, because the road, at that point, is only about two hundred yards from the border fence."

Bradley wanted desperately to forget what had just happened. He knew now that he, most definitely, would *never* talk to anyone about what happened. He could not believe it himself. He was also very determined that under no circumstances would he ever dial the phone number to (the man he now considered to be) Satan. Cannibalism? No thank you. He felt that he would rather spend the rest of his life eating raw rabbit than to ever think of devouring any portion, small or large, of any human anatomy. The thought was just too disgusting. His entire body shuddered in disgust again.

26

A few weeks later, Bradley was called to the Commander's Officer again. He headed over there wondering just what could have gone haywire now. He had kept his mouth shut. He had not told anyone a thing regarding his escapade in Russia. He had also kept his mouth shut about the offer from Bates. What now?

Instead of having to report to the Commander, he was told to go to the First Sergeant's Office. That was usually something better – or not.

He knocked on the open door. "Chief Mathers, you wanted to see me?"

Mathers looked up. "Yes, Sergeant Dooley, I have an extension to your enlistment here. It requires your signature."

Bradley frowned. "But, Chief...I didn't put in for any extension."

"No, you didn't. But, whenever you get a promotion, you are required to wear that rank for a minimum of two years. Your current enlistment is seventeen months short. Once you put on Staff Sergeant, you would only have seven months left, so, you have to extend for seventeen more months...in order to properly accept the promotion."

Bradley contemplated for a moment. "What...if I turn down the stripe?"

Mathers snickered. "Too late."

Bradley nodded and sighed. "All right, Chief, where do I sign?"

"Before you do…" He picked up a small note on his desk. "I have a strange message here…" He looked up frowning. "According to this, a man named Bates, says that he can get that seventeen months waivered. All you have to do is call him and he'll get it taken care of…and you don't have to worry about a thing."

Bradley could not sign the extension fast enough. No to Bates. Yes to the Air Force. "By the way, Chief, I understand as a Staff Sergeant, I get a private room?"

"Yes, of course, that's standard protocol."

"So who has to move? Do I move or does the Kalamazoo Kid have to move?"

Mathers chuckled. "Remember, you're going to be the ranking one. You are the one who decides who moves. Rank doth have its privileges."

"So, I'm notifying you, and I'll notify him…that *he* has to move."

"If that is your decision on the matter – I accept it, because you are the ranking man. Hopper will have to move."

"How soon?"

"As a Staff Sergeant *Selectee*, you already have the clout, even though you haven't put the rank on. You can demand that Hopper start moving…today."

Bradley grinned. "I might just consider staying in...even longer than seventeen months."

Mathers smiled. "Again, that is your decision. That one, however, can wait for a couple of years."

Bradley sighed. "Anything to avoid Bates." He departed the office leaving Mathers frowning over that enigmatic statement.